ALYSSA

THE HALDRED CHRONICLES

ALYSSA

J.G. CULLY

Boyle
&
Dalton

Paperback ISBN: 978-1-63337-279-5
E-book ISBN: 978-1-63337-280-1
LCCN: 2019906409

Manufactured and printed in the United States of America

Dedicated to my friends and family.
Thank you for believing in me.

"They may slay my mortal body, but I am not so easily defeated. Time is on my side, and I will spend it well."

ATTRIBUTED TO IGOR REGORASH

CHAPTER 1
A CLUMSY START

Not again...

This was the first thought that came to Alyssa's mind as she hurtled through the air. She had yet to learn, even after such a long time, how to judge distances properly: a critical requirement for leaping from building to building.

Why me?

That was always the question that came to her mind as she was about to impact.

She adjusted her glasses during her brief mid-air plummet. She expertly twisted her body around so she could land on her back. This was one manoeuvre she had learned to do and do well; she'd had a lot of practice.

With a loud thump, Alyssa landed. She lay flat on her back, gazing up at the moonlit sky, winter clouds drifting lazily past.

"Ouch," she managed in a tiny voice.

Her body was intact; the fall hadn't broken any bones or scratched any skin. She could feel some pain, but it was an uncomfortable kind as opposed to debilitating, as if she had just tripped and fallen on her back instead of having dropped three stories directly onto a cobbled street.

Still pigging hurts, she thought.

She sighed, twisting her head to gaze up at where she had meant to be after her jump: a sizeable ledge jutting from the side of the house opposite. It was a ledge leading to a bottle glass window, the expensive kind. She knew that through the window was a lavishly decorated and pointlessly huge bedroom, and sleeping in the bedroom was a very rich and exceedingly evil man by the name of Ivan McLanan.

Her tongue found her canine teeth; self-consciously she licked at their unnatural sharpness.

It's not evil drinking a crime boss's blood, she reminded herself again. *We'll not kill him. He'll feel terrible in the morning and maybe, just maybe, he'll be more likely to make a mistake. Which will get him in prison. Which will make life better for someone.*

With an accompanying groan, she pulled herself into a seated position, hugging her knees. Gazing upwards, she pulled a strand of her jet-black hair out of her face, her sharp bottle-green eyes considering the ledge.

I guess I'll just have to climb then.

She wasn't sure if climbing was all that practical; her pale blue dress, whilst correctly cut to her figure, was not meant for the wear and tear of nightly roof-running. Neither was she sure she could find purchase against the bricks whilst climbing the wall with the black leather walking shoes she had on, which were not designed for hiking up the sides of buildings, especially in the wintertime.

Leaping in a dress wasn't all that practical either, she mused.

At least this time she hadn't screamed her way down to earth. Her experience of falling off buildings had become so regular that she saw no need to announce it to all and sundry.

At least no one heard me.

"Are you all right?"

"Ah!" she yelped, snapping her head round to the source of the voice.

Standing a few metres away was a young man. He stood with his back to the door of the building Alyssa had unsuccessfully attempted to leap from.

Did he see me fall?

Discovery meant death. Alyssa had accepted that she was in some way already dead, but she'd no great wish to experience it again.

Yet after a few tense seconds, she realized that the guy before her didn't seem to be reacting the way someone would after having just seen a woman hurtling from the sky to land heavily on the ground. He was just standing, seemingly contemplating her. It was only then that she remembered she was still sitting on the ground, in the middle of the street, on a cold winter night.

She stood up quickly, smiling awkwardly.

"Sorry," she said. "I kind of tripped and fell."

"Oh right," the man replied, returning the smile. "Are you okay?"

If only you knew, she thought.

Even though he was standing in the shadows of the door, out of the glare of the street's oil lanterns, she could see him well enough.

3

ALYSSA

He'd a youthful face, with the faintest whiff of a moustache under his nose. His light brown hair was cut short, and he had tender brown eyes, visible to her even in the gloom. *Probably a dockyard worker or something similar,* she reasoned, considering his attire: a brown leather tunic over leggings of the same colour. He had an odd symbol on his left breast pocket, stitched into the fabric in yellow—two jagged circles overlapping one another.

He's handsome, too.

"Yes, I'm okay," she hurriedly blurted out, catching herself staring. "Just tripped, like I said."

"All right." He was staring at her, a slender smile on his face as if distracted.

To Alyssa, this wasn't too unusual. Although she hadn't seen a mirror in over a year and a half, she was reasonably sure she was still what most would consider in the current day and age *pretty.*

"You from around here?" he asked.

Stranger and stranger.

It had been a very long time since she'd had a proper conversation with a human being that didn't start or end with the frantic words, "I have to go now!" Instead, he was looking straight at her and not flinching away. Neither was he hurriedly trying to open his door or anything that would indicate that he wanted to avoid her.

"No." She shrugged and began to relax a little, then flicked her locks back behind her ears, fixing her glasses before speaking again. She found his awkward smile now transitioning to a warmer one. "I'm from farther north. You lived here long yourself?" she asked, gesturing to the man's house.

4

"Yeah." He bobbed his head. "It's not much but it'll do."

The house was a decent size as far as she could see, just a little larger than her own. It was three stories high, built from red muddy bricks with faded but well-kept wooden beams crisscrossing its surface.

Much like most of the buildings in the capital, it was built to space-restricting specifics and squeezed in wherever there was room. Even in the richest areas, space was at a premium, none more so than the Spelgan area.

"It's nice," she said and meant it.

They gazed at each other again.

"Ah," he said at length. "I know this is really forward but… do you want to come in for a cup of tea?"

Alyssa was taken aback, blinking in genuine amazement.

He wants to have tea with me? That better not be some kind of euphemism for sex.

She paused to study him for a moment. If he did try any funny business, she was quite sure she could take him.

Why not?

"Actually, that would be lovely," she decided.

Her smile grew, as did his.

☩ ☩ ☩

She was immediately impressed as he held the door open for her and she entered. The house was indeed as clean on the inside as it was on the outside.

"Have a seat." He indicated the small wooden dining table and chairs at the centre of the room.

She duly sat down, hands clasped in front of her as she gazed around.

A cloak rack sat beside the door with only the man's grey cloak now hanging from it. The floor was unfinished wood, with a few rugs here and there. Mostly plain single-colour rugs, nothing fancy.

The room was tidy. A low bookshelf sat under one of the two small bottle glass windows at the front of the house, stacked with some plain books. A writing table was below the other window, quill and inkwell at the ready and several parchments sitting in uniform lines.

He can afford books and ink. This guy has coin, no doubt about it.

On one wall was arrayed a most unusual sight to Alyssa's eyes. Hung from hooks and shelves was a vast collection of clean metal tools and rings of forged metal, in a similar style to the twinned symbols on his tunic. They were in a bewildering variety of different colours and styles, glinting bronze, copper and iron in the weak light of an oil lantern he had set aflame as they'd entered.

Bemused and intrigued, Alyssa now found her eyes drawn toward the kitchen area. She could see there a fine porcelain sink sitting off to one side with a covered bucket underneath it; a variety of small cupboards were mounted on the walls. Shelves on either side had kitchen implements hanging from them or sitting atop.

He was by the sink now, using the bucket to fill a thermal kettle.

The "*outbreak of peace*" had made a lot of inventions available to the populace of Argon, ones previously confined solely to military use. The thermal kettle, a part-magical device that boiled water, was just one. Possession of a thermal kettle was further indication that her host wasn't poor.

The kettle hissed as he set it aflame by rubbing the heat stone beneath it. He then turned toward her, smiling again. She decided she liked his smile.

"So," he began. "What's your name?"

"Alyssa," she said, finding herself adjusting her glasses once more.

There were a few seconds of silence save for the kettle hissing, during which they stared at each other.

"And you are?" she prompted.

"Sorry!" he started, jumping as if from a trance. "James. James is my name. Sorry, you're a bit distracting…I mean I was a bit distracted!"

She chuckled. "You've not done this often, have you?" she asked, trying to offer him some reassurance as he blushed.

He sighed, some of the tension lifting. "No, I really haven't," he admitted.

"You're in good company." She looked away for a moment. "It's been a while for me too. You can relax."

His relief manifested itself in a softer smile. "I find it difficult to believe someone as beautiful as you hasn't been in a situation like this more often."

She felt her cheeks burning. "Thanks," she replied more shyly, wiping her face in a vain attempt to hide her discomfort.

"Sorry. I've embarrassed you. I only meant to speak the truth."

Alyssa smirked. "And now you've embarrassed me even more!"

ALYSSA

They both laughed.

He hadn't run off; he'd started a conversation with her; he'd even invited her into his house, and *now* he was flirting with her! *Humans don't just flirt with me! But…he is.*

The kettle chose that moment to start to sing with a harsh whistle, as the device reached boiling point.

Leaving her to continue blushing, James poured two cups of steaming black tea, with an aroma of peppermint. As Alyssa recovered, she noticed they were no ordinary cups he had set before her. Porcelain, not wood; Magra imports. He sat directly opposite her at the table.

"So, James," she said, flicking her hair back, "what do you do?"

He hesitated for a moment but nodded, as if confirming something to himself. "Engineering."

Alyssa nodded. "You work with the Machines?"

"Yes indeed."

"That explains…" She waved to the wall with the many tools arranged across it.

"My tools," he agreed. "I'm an apprentice Cog Smelter, first class."

"Cogs!" She pointed at the symbol on his tunic, smiling in recognition. "That's what those are. Sorry, I couldn't remember when I saw them. They run the, what are they called, engines?" "Yes, that's right." He smiled.

"Is it good?" she asked next, taking her cup and sipping from it; she could pretend to like it, even though the liquid could do nothing for her body,

"It's good. The new science is…interesting work. Steam power." He paused. "I don't want to bore you."

"No, please." She motioned with her cup. "I don't know much about it."

"It's…it's kind of like magic sometimes, I suppose. They've used it to move cannons and rams during the war. Then came the siege engines and the bigger siege engines…" He breathed out. "It was messy for a while, but at least now we're using it for better things."

"No more war," Alyssa offered.

"No more war," James agreed. "I'm so glad it's over."

Alyssa nodded. "It was bad for a long time, wasn't it?"

"Fifty years, I think? My father and grandfather both died…" He stopped himself. "Apologies, a little over-sharing."

"It's okay," she reassured him, then changed the subject. "Where were you when the peace was declared?"

He grinned. "Studying. I was just finishing my degree. So glad they still took me on, the dockyards that is. I could have been out without a job. You?"

Alyssa paused. "I was working." Her eyes flickered to her right. "Just…working."

"What do you do?" he asked.

"Barmaid," she said automatically, though with just a touch of hesitation.

"Oh? Which tavern?"

Alyssa smiled inwardly. "Elk's Horn," she said with a touch of pride.

"I know it." He nodded. "I've a few friends that go. Do you enjoy it?"

"Yes. Lots of customers. Lots of variety, we take all races. We've a nice mix."

ALYSSA

Relaxed now, the two of them sat in silence. Drinking tea. She chanced a glance outside, through the front window. It was still dark, but her internal clock was telling her not to delay.

The sun is not your friend, she thought.

She'd found this out with brutal clarity when she'd watched her master, the creature who had transformed her, executing one of his lieutenants by throwing the man into a shaft of sunshine; the man had exploded into a fireball right in front of her, his whole body disintegrating into ash.

She had finished her tea and now felt conflicted. He seemed to notice her nervousness.

"I can tell you want to head home." His sadness was almost tangible.

"No, no," she said immediately. She found her hand suddenly on his in an automatic effort to reassure him. She caught her breath, biting her lip. "It's just been a long night. But I really want to see you again," she blurted out, her hand shooting to her mouth immediately after.

I'm such a child!

"Great," he managed, after several long seconds of surprise.

"Ah." Her eyes flickered again. "Ah, well, why don't you pop in to the Elk's Horn tomorrow night? We could chat during my break?"

"That would be…great," he said hesitantly.

She rose, slowly, and James stood with her.

"Strange times, eh?" she suggested.

He grinned, relaxing. "But good times," he admitted.

She gave him a grin back.

He led her to the door and they both stood looking at each other for a while. He, at the door, not wanting to close it; she, just outside it, not wanting to leave.

It started suddenly. She felt it: a darkening; a sudden terrible feeling of foreboding deep in her stomach. She felt sick, as that feeling rose up within her.

No, no not now, please!

Her eyes widened; she was aware of her pupils dilating; they were drawn toward his neck. She balled her hands into fists, feeling herself tremble. Her breathing quickened.

"Are you alright?"

She ignored him, ignored the meat thing, the living one.

No…must.

Feed.

The word was a scream in her mind. It was a command, a yearning. Her chest tightened.

I will feed later; I am the master of the Craving; I am the director of my actions; I will feed later; I will keep control; I will…

She chanted inwardly as a redness enveloped her view of the world, slowly from the edges of her vision. An inky blood mist, tunneling her vision toward the source of blood…the blood she needed now…craved.

She closed her eyes, squeezing them shut. She heard him speaking again, felt his arms on her shoulders. Felt the urge to let go, to open her eyes.

To feed upon him, to drink upon his…

ALYSSA

And then, it was gone.

She gasped as if coming up for air and fell into his arms.

"I'm okay!" she said, in between gulps of air.

"What was that?" he asked.

She glanced up at him and found his face aghast as she caught her breath. "Seizure," she lied, then swallowed. "It's okay...just give me a moment."

She breathed in and out, her heart hammering in her chest, her body shaking. He kept a tender hand on her shoulder as she regained her composure.

Worst timing ever!

She laughed despite the situation.

"Worst timing ever," she said out loud this time; this made him smile. Composing herself as her breathing returned to normal, she sighed and hugged him.

"Sorry, that...that happens sometimes. Don't worry."

When she let him go, he was smiling.

"Thanks," she said. "You've been kind. Little early though for me to show you at my worst."

"It's all right, I swear. I know some of what you're going through."

I bet you don't.

"Sorry, it has been a long night for me." Alyssa leaned forward and kissed him on the cheek. "Thanks," she added.

He blinked, hand going to where she had kissed him.

"You can stop that now," she remarked, raising an eyebrow.

"Sorry," he answered, quickly forgetting himself.

"See you tomorrow. You can tell me more about cogs and such." She reluctantly started off, then glanced back to see him still at the door, watching her go. They waved to each other. Only when he closed the door did she step into an alcove.

She leant back against the cold stone wall, sighing in relief and wiping sweat from her brow.

That was too close.

For long moments she steadied herself, taking in air, resting her hands that still trembled a little, even curling her toes in her shoes.

The Craving. That could have been unpleasant. She glanced back at James's door. *Let's hope you never realize how close you came.*

She breathed out, and instead, tried to consider the positives of her night. "I just got flirted with," she announced out loud.

She smiled broadly to no one, hugging herself. She hopped from one foot to another. "That was lovely."

"Are you all right, Miss?"

Alyssa almost leapt out of her skin, suddenly pushing herself against the wall. She found herself staring at two Larrick City militia men on the street, their round-rimmed metal helmets and red and blue padded jerkins identifying them, each holding a lantern.

They were frowning at her, heads cocked to one side, eyes narrowed as they scrutinized her.

"Sorry!" she stammered. "I just, ah, the guy."

Both seemed wary of her, exchanging glances.

"I just got flirted with!" she blurted out.

"Okay," said the older one after tense seconds, his frown deepening on his grizzled features.

She suspected that they, unlike James, would not be quite so inclined to kindness. She took a step forward to check. Sure enough, both of them recoiled, hands automatically going to the swords on their belts.

"I'll just be going then."

She quickly turned on her heel, moving off at a quick trot before either of them could enquire further. She could feel them watching her as she left, with hands, she strongly suspected, still on weapons.

Shame, would have been nice if things had changed.

Quickly she turned a corner and was out of sight. She checked the night sky: still dark.

Always darkest before the dawn. Best to hurry off then.

✝ ✝ ✝

Constable Davin Walis and Constable Shane Barnsby watched her go.

"You felt it too, didn't you?" asked Shane, turning to his younger colleague.

"Yeah," he said quietly, finally relaxing the grip he had on the hilt of his sword and lowering the lantern. "That girl…she wasn't right." He swallowed, licking his lips. "Do we report anything?"

Shane grimaced. "Mate, we don't report 'feelings'." He slapped the other constable on the arm. "Come on, forget her. We've got to get to watch house eleven. Get ourselves something warm to eat before we head to the Mounds Pathway."

They trudged off into the night.

Neither one of them was aware of the eyes watching them from the rooftops.

CHAPTER 2

CHANCE ENCOUNTERS

Alyssa's night was not over. She came upon an all-too-common post-war situation in her home city as she rounded a corner.

There, in an alleyway off Holt Street, she saw a very fat, ugly man in mucky work clothes with his hands around the throat of a young and completely terrified girl in an amber dress.

"Let her go!" Alyssa shouted, glowering at the brute, infusing her voice with a certain commanding power. Unfortunately, it seemed the hulk of a man before her was rather drunk; even from a distance, she could smell alcohol. Her power wasn't working.

"Blah haha!" he slurred, letting go of the girl regardless, but now turning his formidable bulk toward Alyssa. "Wa's thes? Annather girly? You's stay aut ah this. Me and her gonna ave sum fun!"

The girl was backing away down the alley on all fours, her frightened breath misting in the cold night air, her face white with fear.

ALYSSA

Alyssa took an authoritative step forward, and the drunk reacted by pulling his right hand back threateningly.

"Ga outta it!" he growled. His meaty hand lashed out.

For Alyssa, time seemed to slow down. The back of the heavy-set drunk's hand hurtled toward her, yet she regarded it with mild disinterest. Even as details of the attacker's paw came into focus, the black hairs and small scars crossing the skin; even as it promised a black eye or even a broken jaw, Alyssa didn't seem the least bit concerned.

Fast as a lightning bolt, her hand shot up, a blur of focused action. With more strength than a young woman of her size or stature had any right to command, she stopped the drunk's arm dead in mid-swing.

He blinked, confusion and shock written plainly on his ugly features. Alyssa allowed herself an evil grin. Before he could do anything else, she brought her other hand up and grabbed the man's elbow. She then twisted and pushed his arm round behind him at a painful angle.

"Grah!" he managed.

"My guardians always said you have to beat manners into a boy," Alyssa whispered in his ear. Her voice dropped an octave. "Here's how."

She grabbed the back of his head with her free hand and slammed his forehead straight into a wooden storage crate stacked by the alley wall. The box burst open, splintering apart, and one very unconscious drunk collapsed to the ground.

Alyssa turned to find the damsel she had just saved staring at her in mute shock.

"Ah," Alyssa said. "Hey."

"Hey," the girl managed in a whisper, her ice-blue eyes wide and watery with tears.

This close, Alyssa could see the girl was no older than her, maybe sixteen. She had long blond hair in curls, which were now messy and lank. She would have been beautiful at any other time, had her face not been so traumatized.

"Are you okay?" Alyssa asked, taking a tentative step forward. She was ready for the girl to bolt; she was entirely unprepared for the real response. "Oof!" Alyssa grunted, as the youngster leapt forward and hugged her tight, burying her face in Alyssa's chest.

"Thank you!" she practically screamed, sobbing. "I was so scared. Thank you. Thank you!"

Alyssa made to speak but she just managed a few indistinct noises. "You're welcome?" she hazarded after a few seconds, though it was a little hard to speak; it was a tight hug. The girl continued to sob into Alyssa's chest.

"Hey," Alyssa said, looking down and stroking the blond strands of the girl's hair. "It's okay, it's over now, all right?"

After a few moments, they stopped embracing each other, the young girl starting to calm.

"What's your name?" Alyssa asked, as the girl's sobbing abated.

"Katy," she said with a sniff, wiping her eyes.

"Katy, I'm Alyssa. Are you going to be okay?"

"Yeah." She flicked her long mane back, trying to fix it. "Gods," she sniffed. "I'm such a mess."

"Could have been worse...much worse."

"Yes, if not for you." She smiled up at Alyssa. She was still trembling. "Thank you so much."

"Right place, right time," agreed Alyssa with a shrug. She secured her glasses before peeking out of the alley, glancing up and down the street. Despite the commotion they had caused, not another soul was in sight; the city was fast asleep. "Where you headed, Katy?"

"Just home, I guess." She swallowed before casting an arm down the street. "I live down the Barnsburn."

"That's not too far. How about I escort you?"

That seemed to straighten the youngster, and she nodded enthusiastically. Alyssa gave the unconscious, inebriated man a glance. "Just do one thing for me. Wait outside the alley for a sec."

"Oh?"

"Just going to tie this guy up, you know; leave him for the militia."

"Oh, right." Katy nodded. Alyssa fancied the girl was all too happy to leave the scene.

Once Katy was safely out of sight, Alyssa turned to the unconscious drunk. She knelt over him.

This time, she let the Craving have its way.

Kneeling by his throat, she opened her mouth. Anyone watching would have observed a horrible transformation. Her canine teeth morphed and elongated. Her fangs extended with a sound not unlike a cat hissing, canine teeth jutting forth from her upper jaw and forming into pin-sharp points. They were long, reaching past her chin. Her upper lip had curled back, and it was as if her whole jaw now jutted forward.

She had no need to heed the prompting of the red mist that encompassed her vision; she knew what to do. Without hesitation, she plunged the tips of her protruding teeth into the man's

18

yielding throat. The blood ran freely. Eagerly, she swallowed it down *through* the fangs, the two bony points draining the blood just above her tongue and down her throat.

She had to stop herself from crying out. The blood flowed; the sensation she felt was pleasure taken to a different level.

I am the master of the Craving; I am...

It was hard to concentrate as her body *willed* her to continue to feed. Demanded it, screeched it into her consciousness. She tried to harden her response.

I...am...

You aren't, came a dark little voice in the back of her mind.

Her eyes, previously closed, shot open. They glinted blood-red in the darkness of the night. Beads of sweat formed on her brow, her hands shaking as she held the unconscious man's shoulders.

I am!

She took control, her grip tightening as she focused.

I am the master of the Craving! I am the director of my actions!

She blinked away her false self, her eyes returning to their human appearance, the pupils and whites shimmering back from beneath the red that had enveloped them so briefly. The blood flow slowed, and she blinked her way out of the sea of emotions and sensations that had stampeded over her. Her breathing slowed. The blood tasted now of only water.

She was done. Alyssa breathed, recovering from her experience.

Quickly she retracted her fangs with a vile-sounding slurp. Her canines, indeed her whole jaw morphed back into her face and her mouth returned to normal. Her eyes fluttered, and then she went to work, to her routine.

19

ALYSSA

She licked the blood from the two minuscule wounds, the better to hide the evidence. By the time the vile man awoke there would be little trace of her act, for the wounds would heal by the morrow. She knew she had to be quick, in case Katy grew suspicious and wondered what she was doing.

"Yuck!" she concluded, wiping the drunk's sweat from her lips. Rubbing her own sweat from her brow, she stood. The contents of her stomach shifted inside her with a groan. She had gorged herself too much; her stomach felt swollen under her dress. Checking that there was no sign of blood on her clothing or her lips, she turned carefully on her heel and left the brute lying on the frozen cobbles.

The girl was waiting for her. "Okay?" Katy asked. She seemed to have calmed down a lot, having even taken time to pull her hair into pigtails.

Bless you, thought Alyssa. "Yeh, well stuffed now." Alyssa grinned.

"Stuffed?" Katy asked.

"Ah, I mean, *he's* well stuffed now," Alyssa stammered, rather quickly removing her hand from her stomach. "You know…once the militia find him."

"Oh right." Katy smiled, after a few seconds of hesitation.

"Anyway," said Alyssa, "lead on."

The two of them started off down the street.

"So, what's your trade?" Alyssa asked, doing her best to cover another bubbling groan coming from her middle.

"Barmaid," Katy replied, rather timidly. "I work at the Hanged Man."

Yikes, thought Alyssa. *The hole cunningly disguised as a tavern.*

"I'm a barmaid, too," Alyssa said. "Though I'm at the Elk's Horn. You're a bit out of your way here, are you not?"

Katy paused before replying. "Actually, I'm looking for new work."

"Oh?"

Katy fidgeted with her blouse sleeves. "The place is a bit scary."

Alyssa nodded. "It does have a reputation." She considered things for a moment. "You're looking for work at this time of the night?" she asked, raising an eyebrow.

Katy sighed, rubbing her arm. "Tonight was a bad night, even before I ran into that guy." She shrugged. "I got a bit desperate, so I started looking for taverns that might still be open."

"Must have been pretty bad." Alyssa reached out, rubbing Katy's shoulder. They walked a little further. They had to keep to the road, as snowdrifts had accumulated on walkways. "You know, we're hiring," she said after a minute, glancing across at Katy.

The younger girl perked up. "You think it could work?"

"No harm in trying. I warn you, a lot of our customers aren't human. That a problem?"

"Not a problem." The girl grinned. "I get on with non-humans. Sometimes I'm mistaken for an elf, which is nice."

Alyssa smiled.

I can see why, apart from the height.

Katy hesitated for a moment. "Except...there aren't any bearkin, are there?" she asked, hesitantly.

Alyssa shook her head. "Nah. The ceiling's too low for them."

Katy appeared relieved. "That's great. They scare me a bit. If you'll take me?"

ALYSSA

"I'll put in a good word," promised Alyssa.

The two chatted the rest of the way. Fortunately for Alyssa, Katy set a brisk pace, so Alyssa didn't find herself worrying about the impending sunlight. They had a great deal in common. Katy enjoyed reading and embroidery, just as Alyssa did, and had an interest in geography, again like Alyssa. They discovered they had attended rival schools. Alyssa even regaled Katy of her time in her orphanage.

"I'm so sorry," she said after Alyssa told her.

Alyssa shrugged. "It's okay, I was lucky. The orphanage where I grew up taught me a lot about living."

They finished the brief walk knowing each other a lot better, the painful experiences of the night giving way to friendship by the time they arrived at Katy's door.

The Barnsburn district was in the east of the city. The houses were dirty red brick, with ageing timbers supporting the walls and shuttered windows instead of modern bottle glass. Signs of do-it-yourself home repairs were everywhere, from wooden boards serving as doors to what appeared to be ship timbers boarding up windows.

"Thank you again, Alyssa." Katy's hand was on the door.

"No bother."

The two of them embraced, Katy hugging Alyssa tightly. Katy frowned as she stepped back, casting Alyssa a worried look.

"What's wrong?" she asked. "Your stomach seems all swollen up."

"Ah, no, no. I'm fine! Just…" Alyssa rubbed her stomach. "…just stress!" she settled on. "You know? Delayed reaction. Scary situation, that sort of thing."

"Oh." Katy shrugged, then smiled. "I hope you sleep off the stress."

"Yeah, I'll be fine."

"Okay. Thank you again. I'll pop into the Elk's Horn tomorrow night?"

Alyssa readily nodded.

"I'm in your debt," Katy said. "You're a really good person."

Alyssa smiled warmly and the two parted ways, Katy waving before entering her house. Alyssa watched her go. It was only when Katy was behind her closed door that Alyssa's face fell. She sighed, scratching the back of her head.

"No, Katy, I'm not a good person," she muttered. "In fact, I'm not even a person anymore."

With that, she checked her glasses again and turned, heading off to her own house as quickly as her overfilled stomach would allow. Around her, it started to snow.

† † †

Katy watched Alyssa go from the small window beside her front door, peering through a crack in the shutters. Alyssa's silhouette was soon swallowed by the flickering snow.

"Everything okay?" her mother asked from behind her, standing in the hallway cleaning a pan with a rag.

"Yeah," Katy said.

There was a pause as her mother yawned. "Who was that?"

"A new friend," Katy replied. She glanced over her shoulder towards her mother. The single lantern burning in the hallway lit Katy's face for a moment. "She's…different," Katy said.

Her mother gazed back. For a moment the two blond women observed each other in the flickering light. *"That* kind of different?" her mother asked.

Katy inclined her head slowly, the motion barely visible in the night time.

Her mother examined the pan she'd been drying before regarding her daughter again. "Just be careful, like always," she advised, before pacing back to the kitchen.

Katy closed the shutters and nodded to herself before making for her bedroom.

☨ ☨ ☨

Alyssa was back at her house in short order. Even as she entered, the first rays of sunlight had started to creep across the horizon, stabbing through the grey clouds heavy with further snow. Having closed the window shutters on her house, she changed into her bedclothes, a fine white nightdress draped over her. She set her glasses on a dresser by her bed, a single candle having been lit beside them.

I'm such a greedy gorb.

She was feeling much like a wine barrel, sluggish and heavy. She decided that laundry and cleaning could wait until tomorrow; she was far too full to care.

She sighed as she sat down on the bed.

New rule. No more fat bad guys.

The change was sudden.

The room dropped in temperature, Alyssa's breath becoming misty. The shadows grew darker, and Alyssa felt an uncomfortable pressure inside her skull. In the far corner, by her wardrobe, a shape was forming. Tendrils of darkness seemed to first erupt from the walls, then retract back, swirling around two red lights that slid into existence, like the embers of some forgotten candle, glinting in the black.

A voice seemed to fill the room, rasping and urgent in its tone, yet it also seemed to boom inside Alyssa's mind.

The blood gives you strength.

Alyssa rolled her eyes. "Hello, Vlad," she said out loud, with a lack of concern at the palpable evil that had come to visit.

Why did you not drain the virgin?

The voice echoed inside Alyssa's head, for that was where Vlad existed. She had named him: the name he had given for himself was, for her at least, impossible to pronounce. It was some ancient vampire language.

Vlad hated the name Vlad. It was one of her ways of getting back at him.

She wasn't sure what he was. A vampire spirit? An undead monster of some kind? A final curse set on her by Igor?

Alyssa did her best to belittle him, using humour to hit back at him. "Just so you know, I've not missed you," she mocked him, regarding the darkened corner. The red lights seemed to frown.

Why did you not drain the virgin? Vlad repeated with greater intensity. *The blood of a virgin is pure and fresh. An elixir capable of enhancing your powers ten-fold.*

"Because I would have burst!" retorted Alyssa. She looked down at the swelling of her stomach, directing Vlad's attention, before glaring back at the cloud of rolling, almost shimmering darkness. "Do you see how bloated I am?"

Vlad chuckled, a rattle of stone upon the mountainside. He preferred it when she was angry.

The physical limitations of the flesh do not apply to you, girl. Ragnor the Ravenous would gorge himself before battle on up to three selected delicacies. He was practically unstoppable.

Vlad seemed to have an encyclopedic knowledge of vampiric history and gloried in reminding Alyssa of every other vampire before her, reminding her of the legacy she unwillingly lived.

"*He* wasn't an eighteen-year-old girl!" she retorted.

Foolish child! he hissed; Alyssa flinched as the pain in her head felt like a spear punching through the back of her head. She was aware of the cloud of darkness growing, encompassing the room. *You cannot escape your legacy. Regorash turned you so you could rule. First Argon, then the world. That, you cannot stop.*

It was not the first time Vlad had demanded she step back on the path of the damned.

How long will you deny your nature? How long will you delay what is already set in motion?

Doing her best to ignore him, Alyssa concentrated on a spot in front of her, imagining a tiny light; a pinprick of white in the black; a solitary flame.

The Six Nations War is at an end. The armies of the great nations are disbanded. Opportunity beckons for those willing to embrace what they are.

Slowly, the light became real, at least to her. She willed it into existence, then willed it to grow. Gradually, it did just that. The flicker of light became a beacon; the beacon became a bonfire.

Time is on my side, girl. You cannot deny me, or your destiny, forever.

Steadily, the room brightened. Where the light touched, the darkness recoiled. The red eyes flinched, and the room filled with a feral growl.

Impressive, but temporary, Vlad spat with malice, though his voice no longer had the intensity nor authority it had once possessed.

The black was pushed away.

Now that she had cast him back into her subconscious, she worked to imprison him. She concentrated hard, thinking of a sturdy box. A chest, metal-lined and built of tough oaken wood. A strongbox with a padlock. She visualized opening the box, allowing the padlock to clatter to the floor. Then, into it, the darkness was poured. Blackened fingers crawled and writhed in her hands as she crammed them into her imaginary box. Finally, the box was filled.

From within, two red eyes regarded her. She was used to this scene, this waking dream, this imagined prison for her partner. Sometimes the red lines seemed to be hating her, other times they seemed to be almost impressed. This time, Vlad just stared at her as she made to close the chest's lid.

Until our next session, Alyssa the Last.

She closed the lid and locked the padlock. He was silenced.

Alyssa opened her eyes. She found her room once again as it was meant to be: in the dark but not in the darkness. She sat for a moment, enjoying the silence. The only light came from the single candle that flickered beside her. Outside, the city was waking up.

A grin started to spread across her face.

James.

ALYSSA

She lay down on her side, still grinning broadly, and grabbed Mr Rabbit to hug him close. "I was flirted with tonight, by a boy," she told him. The expression on the plain stuffed animal remained disappointingly neutral.

She giggled to herself again, before flushing, thinking how much of a child James would think her if he knew what she was doing right now.

Light in the darkness. Just a small light in the darkness. A light I nearly ate.

She shivered at the thought.

That was too close.

She had checked the blackout curtains and her house windows and doors before she had entered her bedroom. All locked tight, all closed and none in a position to let any of the lethal sunlight through. She was safe. She pulled her covers over her head, just in case, and summoned her strength to place her in her *death sleep*.

She imagined herself falling asleep, as she used to when she was alive, but more forced, almost like putting herself into a trance. Slowly, her body would follow her wishes. Slowly but surely, she drifted off.

She knew she was asleep when the dreams began.

✝ ✝ ✝

The large figure stumbled, walking in a zig-zag across the path. On either side of the path were metal spikes. Old defensive obstacles left over from the Six Nations War, they pointed upward and inward, still sharp, still deadly.

He groaned, his hands scratching an itch upon his neck. He shook his head, grunting.

"Stupid girl."

He growled.

"Hit my head…" He lost his footing and fell heavily onto the track. With a grunt, he heaved himself up again.

Two shadows loomed over him in the waxing dawn. "Yes, he will do nicely."

The figure looked up at the voice and swore; he met with cloaked blackness that seemed impossibly tall.

"Wha's tha'?" he slurred, but then quite suddenly felt his body being lifted up. He tried to cry out, but no sound came.

"As you will, Leader," said another voice from beside the first, the glint of metal visible beneath a hood.

Held a few feet off the ground, floating in mid-air, the man was spun and moved over the edge of the path. He tried to struggle but his limbs would not move.

His head was pulled back by some invisible force, exposing his neck.

Slowly, he was lowered. He tried to struggle again, more urgently now, for he found himself being lowered onto one of the spikes.

"Do not worry," came the first voice again, "for you have set in motion events of great import."

"As the Leader wills it," the second voice concurred, "so it shall be."

The forces holding him abruptly disappeared, and the fat man fell hard.

CHAPTER 3

THE HUNTRESS

"Here he is, Clark, one dead fat guy."

The two militia men hauled the body-cart into the laboratory. Clark, the Militia-Sanctioned Mage on duty that morning, grimaced, setting down his mug of Sleep Deprivation Serum and wiping his mouth on his sleeve.

"Just what I wanted for my birthday," Clark remarked without humour, rubbing his temple before pulling his long, greying hair out of his eyes. He stood, straightening his belt and pulling the sleeves of his robe up past his elbows.

"This is Davin; he's new." Shane, the older constable, motioned to his colleague. "He called it in."

There was a certain mocking tone in Shane's voice, a twinkle of mischief in the militia man's emerald eyes and the briefest smirk at the edge of his mouth.

Clark pulled on a set of goggles, securing them to his forehead by a leather strap, before regarding the young man. "You don't think it was an accident?" he asked as he wiped his hands on a towel he grabbed from the bench beside him.

Davin stopped examining the pile of empty ingredient bottles that had been built into a haphazard tower in the corner of the room and shrugged, youthful hazel eyes switching first to his colleague, then to the mage and back again.

"I did at first," he admitted, in a soft voice, unhurried. "But, the wound…" He drew near to the body and pointed to an ugly, deep wound, just under the dead man's chin. "He was impaled on the railings. We should have seen a lot more blood."

Clark had donned his leather butcher's apron. "All right, mate. Is that why the initial report says…" Clark crossed back over to his workbench and picked up a paper. He adjusted his glasses as he surveyed the courier-fey delivered report and read it out.

"*Body discovered halfway between watch houses eleven and twelve, along Mounds Pathway, approximately four foot off the ground. Initial discovery by Constable Walis and Constable Barnsby. Suspected drunk. Concern raised that not enough blood coming from the corpse. Death marked as suspicious.*" Clark let the report drop and peered at Davin.

"Yes," Davin confirmed. "Sorry if it sounds too formal."

Clark hummed to himself. "Are you's getting overtime for this?" he asked pointedly, eyeing the militia men.

"Yes," the constables replied in unison.

Clark smirked. "All right." Removing his glasses and setting them carefully on a table, he pulled his goggles down over his eyes, adjusting the magnification with a dial set into the side of them. He then retrieved some clean metal tools from a nearby drawer: a sharp knife and a short metal rod with a spike at its end.

"Just to clarify, you don't think he just fell?" he asked as he bent to examine the body.

"No," answered Davin.

"Even though the Mounds Pathway is a pigging dangerous place to walk, especially if you're inebriated."

"Sorry?"

Clark stopped, blinking at the younger constable. "Wrote off, son. Banjaxed. Pole-axed."

Davin's frown furrowed, and his eyelids flickered a few times.

"Drunk," Shane finally explained.

"I had a whole list to try, mate," said Clark with a smile.

"I know, but I want to go home," replied Shane, now leaning on the wall, watching. "I prefer my overtime optimized."

"Spoilsport," said Clark.

He used the sharp knife to inspect the most obvious wound first, the one Davin had already pointed out. Beside him, he placed a registration parchment. Occasionally he would stop his inspection and write down his findings with a quill and inkpot.

Check for kill wound and describe: <u>*Present, metal spike to the throat, through lower jaw, immediately fatal.*</u>

"Wish they'd move the damn things," Clark remarked as he finished making his first note. "The spikes, I mean."

"We submitted a request," Davin confirmed.

"Already?"

"Told ye he was keen." Shane chuckled. "Good idea, though. I mean, the war's over, right? Don't need 'em anymore."

"Be interesting to see how quickly they do that," Clark said, making another note.

Check for other injuries: Bruising suggests blunt impact to front of skull. Non-fatal. No additional wounds from external forces visible.

"Did yeah's get a Death Warden?" Clark asked next, casting a wary eye over the rest of the body.

"The death has been officially recorded by the Death Warden's Guild associate," Davin answered.

"Translation, yes," Shane said. "Don't worry, I educated him. Death Wardens for the death, Corpse Wardens for the body afterwards. I mean, they do the same thing but sure!" Shane throw up his hands in exasperation.

"What did he say, the Death Warden?" Clark asked next, seeming to ignore Shane's theatrics.

"He said to ask you," Shane said.

"Lazy sod," Clark said, smirking. He wiped his hands on his towel again. "I don't mind, though. Beats investigating life mages casting spells on people's beards."

"Do they actually do that?" asked Davin, crossing his arms.

"Oh aye." Clark smiled. "Not a great sense of humour, those boys." Clark made another note on his parchment.

Check for signs of disease: none found.

"Right, let's see if your blood theory is right." He replaced his previous knife with an even sharper one, then adjusted his goggles again before bending down to hold a small cup near the man's left hand. He slit the corpse's wrist.

Clark flinched, but he need not have. Only a small dribble of crimson red bled from the wound. "That's not right," he muttered to himself in a low voice.

After some time with his sharp blade, making minute incisions to various parts of the body, Clark wiped his hands again and crossed his arms, frowning. "Bad news, Shane," he said to the older constable.

"What?"

Clark motioned toward Davin. "He's right. That's not normal."

Shane stopped leaning on the wall.

"I've been checking the body over from top to toe," Clark continued, pulling his goggles off his forehead. "And yeah, there's not the kind of blood flow I would expect from an individual of this size, and this fresh."

Shane shrugged. "All right, Davin, I owe you a pint."

"Why is that?" asked Davin, speaking to Clark again. "The blood, I mean."

Clark moved to a cabinet across from them and opened it. Within, various tools glinted. There was a crackle and hum in the air as Clark removed a device. He held it up for the two constables to see. "The Scope," he declared. "Part magic, lads, so if you're not into that kind of thing, I suggest you stand back."

Shane duly did so, though Davin remained near, watching as Clark set to work again.

The Scope resembled an oversized magnifying glass, the glass itself an oddly blue hue. It was ringed in copper and silver, with an odd gemstone set into the handle. Clark waved the device slowly over the body. Davin watched as Clark paused occasionally, peering through the Scope. The hum in the air increased and decreased, always in the background. After some time, Clark stopped. "There we are." He motioned to Davin, who leaned closer.

Through the glass of the device, two wounds appeared upon the body's throat. Tiny, almost ghostly under the device's influence.

Davin did not at first see what Clark noted on his parchment. *Use Scope to check for possible healing potion use: <u>two pinprick wounds revealed via Scope, on victim's throat just above main artery.</u>*

"I'll pass it to the Head of Magical Investigations," Clark said, setting the Scope down. "He'll likely request that the investigation 'be concluded with all haste,' as they say in the trade. Then he'll pass it to the Council of Peace. The body will be taken into care by the other guild, the Corpse Wardens, and they'll do the exact same investigation as me."

"Oh?" Davin asked.

"Well, would you like a big fat mess stinking up *your* lab?" asked Clark.

"No, but…" Davin's face showed worry. "Council of Peace?"

"Oh yes. Vampire, son." Clark pointed to the body's throat. "That's what those two little wounds would suggest, unless you know of a couple of particularly vicious hummingbirds."

"Vampire," the young constable breathed.

"Aye, vampire." Clark exhaled. "That, and the boss is wanting to transfer out of here to the Magic Training and Safety Division."

Shane smirked. "Had enough, has he?"

"Oh yes." Clark nodded. "This'll be his chance. High-profile case, fire it off to the right people and they'll get him shipped off."

Davin was gazing over at the body. "A vampire," he said again.

"Yes, lad, a vampire," Clark agreed.

All three clustered round, regarding the corpse.

"A confirmed threat to peace," the mage concluded.

✝ ✝ ✝

She sighed and leaned back in her plush cushioned chair, blinking. Late morning sunlight was streaming in through the glass window beside her, shining over the papers on her desk; it was her debrief report for another job completed. She read over what she had written again.

Summary of operation:

Renegade Darnhun mercenaries confirmed raiding ships up and down northern coast of Tornar and southern coast of Trima. Several beach villages attacked. Investigator and sanctioned mercenaries dispatched to investigate. Three days tracking required (see attached expenses). Located renegade base on small island, directly east of Tornar. Operation to remove renegades successful, no prisoners required. Merchant ships crews freed. Protests made by Darnhun government. Tornar government and Trima tribal council supportive of Council of Peace operation. Peace maintained.

The last line brought a smile to her face. "Leave the politics to the politicians," she said to herself. She leaned forward again and signed her name.

Victoria Haldred, Council of Peace Investigator

She sat back once more and grimaced; her hands moved to the base of her spine. "Going to have to check that saddle again," she muttered.

She moved her hands to the swell of her hips and rolled her eyes. "So that's where the travel rations were going."

ALYSSA

She stood up, taking the report in hand, and walked over to her office's letter tray. She rolled the parchment up and popped it into the shelf labelled with a wood-carving *completed*; it was full.

Automatically, she looked to the small mirror that was mounted on the back of the office door. Her reflection stared back. She checked her features. Her long black locks were tied back in an elegant braided ponytail, wooden clasps holding it in place. She had plain but unblemished features, close-set blue eyes staring out over a small, pointed nose and similarly small mouth.

"Oh Gods." She grimaced before stepping back from the mirror so that her whole body was visible.

She turned, inspecting her black leggings and burgundy tunic. She straightened, pulling the tunic down so that it sat properly above the black leather belt tied around her middle. Her hand went to the small circular cut of metal emblazoned with her badge of office that was attached beside the belt's clasp. The badge depicted six small circles, one for each of the six nations, all connected toward a stylised hand: the outstretched hand of peace. She made sure it was firmly attached, then nodded to herself. "Yeah," she insisted to her reflection, "better from a distance."

A knock came at the door.

"Come in," she said with disinterest as she returned to her desk.

The door was opened by her partner, Malak. The hawk-faced man poked his head through the door and favoured her with a grin full of clean white teeth. "Bored yet?"

"Get in here, you ass," she ordered, casting him a pitying look. "You're like a little lost schoolboy."

"I live in the Argon capital," he replied, his grey eyes alight with mischief as he moved into the room. He ran a hand over his shaven head. "I am lost."

The skinny Tornarian native slid into the room, despite his full armour array. The leather armour was secured round his chest with a variety of straps and was covered in pouches. Victoria observed that as usual, the thick leather belt around his middle was adorned with a Tornar punch dagger and crossbow bolts for his favoured weapon, a K-12 repeater crossbow. Dark green shirt and leggings, as well as leather grieves, completed his appearance.

The only indication that he even worked for the Council of Peace was a metal clasp, hanging from one shoulder, with the same symbol on it as that on Victoria's belt badge. On the other shoulder was emblazoned a carving in the shape of a bulldog's face.

He handed her a rolled-up parchment as he passed her desk. On it was the Council of Peace wax mark, a stylized "CoP." She snapped the wax mark as Malak took a seat at his desk and started sorting through his paperwork.

"I think I've put on weight," Victoria said. "I think all those rations have gone to my hips."

"Right," Malak said carefully, stopping for a moment, "remind me again, do I say anything about that or just keep quiet?"

Victoria rolled her eyes. "An honest opinion would be appreciated," she suggested.

"No, it wouldn't, not for me anyway."

Victoria was looking over now, glaring at him. "So you think…"

"No, I don't!" Malak replied immediately, concentrating intently on his paperwork.

"Malak." Victoria's voice had lowered, much as a teacher speaking to a disobedient student.

"The last guy to comment on your appearance got a punch in the face." Malak shook his head. "I'm not being the next fella."

Victoria opened her mouth to reply but then closed it again. There was a pause before she spoke. "You think that was an over-reaction on my part?" she said finally.

"He said you had a nice arse." He peered over at her. "He was just complimenting you."

"In a way that made me want to punch him, so I did."

Malak breathed out. "My country still has a lot to learn about your country," he admitted.

He returned to his papers, she to hers.

"In other words, you lot need to learn proper manners," Victoria stated, after a minute.

"This Tornarian," Malak thumbed toward his chest, "has been educated, I can assure you."

Victoria read through the report. "This is something new," she mused, with an accompanying frown, after a few moments of speed reading.

"Oh?" Malak asked, carefully signing another request for flechette crossbow bolts.

"Suspected vampire."

Malak gave her a look of surprise. "Vampire?"

She held up the parchment. "That's what it says." She rolled up the paper again and tossed it across the room to him. He digested the information. Victoria pretended to examine the papers on her desk, watching him out of the corner of her eye, concealing a smirk with her hand when he frowned and shook his head.

"Somebody's taking the piss," he said, with typical bluntness. "Regorash is dead. Proper dead. He was the last."

"Oh yes, the Blood Tyrant," Victoria mused.

"Destroyer of hope, master of evil." Malak shook his head. "Yeah, may as well have put a huge sign around his neck marked 'I'm the bad guy.'"

"You know about Shadowhawk, I take it?" Victoria asked, catching the parchment as Malak tossed it back to her.

"What?"

"That's what they called it," she explained. "The mission to take down Regorash."

"I didn't know the name, but I read about it. You lot sent in some, what were they called, Specialists?"

"Plucky Adventurers is what the people relations people called them." Victoria found herself gazing out the window. "Assassins would have been more accurate."

"Sounded like a hell of an operation." Malak returned to his parchment work. "About half of them killed?"

"Aye," agreed Victoria. "Other half made a fortune on the stories afterwards."

"Saw them advertised on the street market." He stopped for a moment, tapping his forehead. "'My Role in the Big Kill', that was one of them, I think?"

"That's one yes." She nodded. "'Dust and Ash' was the other one, by the bearkin of the group. He's the one who killed him."

"They any good?" Malak had a certain twinkle in his eye.

"*You'd* probably appreciate them." Victoria looked over at him. "I thought they were a bit over the top, to be honest." Then she mused, "There were some pigging awful songs as well."

"Oh?"

"'I'll Beat Your Face in, Ye Fanged Monkey' and 'What About Ye, Ye Blood-sucking Cesspit.'"

Malak was aghast. "Those are *songs?*"

"I know." Victoria shook her head. "Not our finest musical accomplishments. Popular in a couple of the taverns, though.

"They can do a lot of damage," Victoria said next. "Vampires, I mean."

"Oh aye?"

"Regorash pretty much set up his own pocket empire." She started to examine the report again. "Wiped out about a dozen villages, Gods only know how many he killed. From what I've read, he was on the cusp of launching a siege of Larrick City." Victoria frowned. "They're dangerous. Shadowhawk was necessary. Six Nations War was still going on, we couldn't fight another war on our doorstep."

"You had no choice," Malak agreed. He was warming to the conversation. "Trima were breathing down your necks. Magra were well up for continuing the war. Thank the Gods for the Wappa."

Victoria raised an eye. "Wappa?"

"World Wide Peace Agreement," Malak clarified.

"Where did you hear it described that way? Wappa doesn't even fit, it should be Wepa or..."

"It's what Doris down in the Diplomacy office calls it." Malak interrupted.

Victoria shook her head again. "Poor Doris, didn't have her down for acronyms, or whatever that was." Victoria again stared off across the open window, crossing her arms thoughtfully. "The signature's from Overseer Gladwell," she said. "He wouldn't pass this down if it didn't warrant at least looking into."

Malak raised his head to give her a wary eye. "I don't know about that fella."

"I know." Victoria made a face. "Not exactly the nicest creature to ever grace the Council of Peace recruitment drive."

"How the hell did such a man even get that job?"

Victoria raised her arms in defeat. "Don't know. I will openly admit to you, there are some aspects of this country and this organization I do not understand, and kind of don't *want* to understand. Politics."

"You lot have too much of it," Malak said, mockingly. "Councillors, and senators, and master-councillors…"

"We do have to do this," Victoria interrupted her colleague's monologue.

Malak groaned from the corner. "Gods, woman," he groaned. "You're going to make me ride again, aren't you?"

"You see, that's another thing I don't understand about you, Malak." Victoria turned to him. "You lot *invented* the concept of light cavalry. Why do *you* hate horses?"

"I don't hate horses." Malak raised a hand in defense. "I just don't like riding the damn things. I prefer my feet on the ground, not wrapped around the middle of an animal, which might not necessarily like me."

"Nasty childhood?"

"Don't want to talk about it." He lowered his head.

"We're not riding this time, you'll be glad to hear," she said, ceasing her contemplations and standing stiffly. "We'll take the coach this time."

Malak frowned. "What? Right now?"

"We can satisfy your obsession with crossbow ammo later, Malak," she teased. "According to this, the victim is still fresh. You really want to leave the smell to get any worse?"

Malak grunted but stood nonetheless. "Fair point."

Victoria unhooked her rapier from the wall beside her: a fine Tornarian blade with attached sword catcher, sheathed in brown leather. Feeling the reassuring weight of her favourite weapon, she secured the rapier to her belt before opening her desk drawer and grabbing the black powder pistol and leather holster that lay within. She checked the Argon-built single shot, flicking the breech open and checking inside.

"You clean it?" enquired Malak.

"Yes, I did," Victoria replied, with a hint of pride.

With a flick of her wrist, the weapon closed again, and Victoria admired the gold trim that coiled around the weapon's steel barrel and polished wooden stock. She pulled the hammer back, checking the flint, before pulling the trigger and hearing the reassuring click as the hammer leapt forward.

"Bit showy," Malak observed.

"Shut up, Malak," Victoria replied automatically, as he smirked.

Malak grabbed his treasured K-12 off the back of his chair. He worked the locking mechanism on the Tornar-built repeater crossbow before sighting down the weapon's length. He flexed the pull-string carefully before sliding out the box of bolts within the weapon, checking the contents.

"You really do love that thing," Victoria commented, making sure all her assorted equipment and weapons were secured on her person.

"Her name is 'Bess' and she is a fair lady indeed."

He plugged the box of bolts back into the underside of the weapon, flicking the locking mechanism back to its neutral position on the underneath of the stock. Inside, there was a faint whirl of clockwork. His final act was to run his hand along the considerable number of notches on the side of the weapon. "Not her fault her chosen profession is war," he concluded.

Victoria raised an eyebrow. "You are an odd fish, aren't you?"

Malak slung his crossbow before replying. "Says the woman who joined the Council of Peace on day one."

"What can I say?" She spread her arms wide in a mocking gesture before moving for the door. "They needed me." All set, Victoria motioned to the door. "After you."

"Nah, after you," said Malak, making a similar motion. "It's only polite."

Victoria coughed. "Malak, the only reason Tornar men let a woman walk through doors in the first place is so they can admire them, and as you have so recently clarified, I have a…"

Malak cleared his throat. "Fine arse," he stated, reluctantly. "Yeah."

"In my defence," Malak responded, moving to comply with his colleague's order, "I didn't say that originally, I was just repeating…"

"Get out."

"Yes, ma'am."

They headed out.

ALYSSA

"Please tell me we can burn this one soon."

It was the Corpse Warden's opening comment.

They had left their department's stone-clad building in the early afternoon and arrived at the militia morgue in just under an hour. The streets, as always, had been packed, but the Council of Peace-registered coach they rode in was built for the streets of Larrick City. It was narrowly constructed, perfect for sliding through the tight laneways of the city.

They were met at the morgue by one of the Corpse Wardens, the guild responsible for body disposal.

"A Death Warden tells you how the recently deceased became recently deceased." Victoria let the representative explain things to Malak as he led them into the building. "A Corpse Warden has responsibility for the body afterwards. So, we get the fun job." His name was Garrett and his accent was northern Argon, his speech fast but clear.

They were in the morgue now, the area cleared of all but the body they had come to investigate. Each of them wore face cloths filled with herbs to protect them from the smell of death that lingered in the air. Even so, Victoria and Malak were still uncomfortably aware of it. The morgue had plain stone-bricked walls dug out of the earth, much like an underground temple or burial chamber. A single stone slab sat at the centre with a desk beside it, arrayed with a variety of savage and unusual instruments, both engineered and magical. Sharp-looking knives, saw blades, and punch-daggers, as well as odd-looking gemstones set into plates of metal or wood, and a large blue-glass magnifier. Light was provided by a shaft of sunlight through an opening in the ceiling.

Garrett led them over to the body, wiping his hands on his priestly robes of blue.

Whilst it was currently winter and bodies did not decompose as quickly as in summer, the body in question was not a pleasant sight, even with a thick sheet of white cloth draped over it.

"Here he is," Garrett said. Idly, he picked up a magnifying glass, then stooped to use his free hand to pull back the sheet of cloth. "First thoughts, the fat sow fell and impaled himself." He held up the magnifying glass over the large wound under the body's jaw. "Spiked railing," he said, adjusting his thick glasses. "Straight into him and right on up into his brain. Death was instant. The militia report was accurate." He let the cloth drop and turned back toward them. "Questions?"

"Stupid one first," Victoria offered, casting a cautious eye over the corpse. "Does it seem like murder?"

"Unlikely." There was a professional confidence evident in his northern Argon tone. "He fell off the Mounds Walkway. That place is hazardous to your health without the piggin' spikes, let alone with. Granted, he's the first to have died, but only just. Others have been lucky enough just getting their arms or legs spiked through. Nasty."

"Could he have been thrown?"

"With the precision of the impact point?" Garrett shook his head, rubbing his stubby chin. "Nah. I wouldn't like to have been the one to try and pick this guy up. Even the contract ogres had difficulty moving him in."

"So, you think he was just unlucky?" Malak suggested next.

Garrett nodded before running a hand over his balding scalp. "And I'd still think so if it weren't for what else was found."

"The bite marks," Victoria said.

Garrett picked up an ornate magnifying glass from his table, pulling the cloth back again to reveal just the body's neck. "Invisible to the naked eye," he said, "but not to this mage thing." He beckoned them closer and held the glass over a section of the neck.

Victoria leaned in to watch, somewhat more hesitantly than Malak.

The blue-tinged glass did not change at first, seeming just like the lens of the other magnifier. But then, as they watched, the wounds became visible, as if materialising over the corpse's throat. Two tiny pin-pricks, hardly visible even under the magical magnifying glass but there nonetheless, positioned more or less an inch apart and at the same level. "That," Garrett went on, "added to the lack of blood in the body upon death, is presumably why this case found its way to you lot."

Victoria cast Garrett a knowing glance.

"I'm well read," he said, in answer to the look. "I know the stories."

"Who figured out the lack of blood?" asked Victoria next, leaning back and crossing her arms, frowning as Garrett set the spyglass down again.

Garrett smiled. "New kid with an eye for promotion. He's the son of a long-running line of detectives and seems to have inherited his father's knack of seeing the unusual. I think this will be the making of him, get him off the street and doing what you lot do."

"Poor lad doesn't know what he's in for," said Malak, mournfully.

"Anything else?" Victoria asked.

"Aye," Garrett said. "One other odd thing was the evidence of impact to the front of the skull. It appears he banged his head pretty bad. No fractures but severe bruising. Would have been enough to knock him out, I think."

"The ass probably banged his head off a bloody door," grunted Malak.

"Enough to knock him out? So, he would have been unconscious some of the night?" Victoria mused.

"Maybe about fifteen minutes, maybe less," Garrett said. "We didn't think much of it. I mean, the guy was pissed, didn't even need the mages to tell us that. You could bloody smell it off him. Other than that, and the kill-wound, there's nothing else."

"You got the report?" Victoria asked, after examining the body again, a frown deep upon her forehead.

Garrett duly recovered the report from a drawer in his desk. "Keep it for as long as you need. All the details are in there, including times and figures. Just make sure to sign for it on your way out and bring it back when you're done."

Victoria nodded.

"Can I burn him now?" asked Garrett, with a smile.

Victoria nodded again. "I think we have all we need. Thank you."

"No bother."

☩ ☩ ☩

"It's bull," Malak stated.

They were back in the coach, trundling through the streets again to meet with the militia troops who had discovered the body. The winter sun was low; the sky was clear and the temperature was cold, both Victoria and Malak's breath misting as they talked. The streets were busy with merchants out in force and people going about their business through the partially snow-covered streets, unaware of the recent murder in their midst.

"Malak, your canine teeth are about an inch apart," Victoria stated, pointing to his mouth. "And the two wounds were the same width apart on the body. Right where the artery is. Right where the blood flows. Add that to the lack of blood in the body and you might not have a definitive case, but you do have the beginnings of one."

Malak rolled his eyes. "He was a drunk. A seasoned drunk. You any idea what that amount of drink can do to a man?"

"I don't but I bet you do," Victoria said with a knowing smirk.

"He ate badly and drank heavily," continued Malak, ignoring her jab. "Lack of blood is probably just part of that. And as for the wounds?" He screwed up his face. "Clutching at straws."

"I always love the way you just discard evidence, Malak," Victoria said, without humour, "just because you can't explain it. Besides, I know the real reason why you're grumbling." She gazed out at the passing streets. "You fear this is one of those cases where you don't get to shoot anything." She cast him a disappointed look. "Would I be right?"

Malak didn't answer.

"Patience," she advised, returning her gaze to the window. "If there is a vampire out there, you might just be the one who takes the first shot at it."

CHAPTER 4

AN UNFORTUNATE
TURN OF EVENTS

Alyssa stretched as she awoke.

It had been a nice dream. James had been in it, her soon-to-be boyfriend. She hoped. Katy too, her new friend. Both of whom she met on the same night.

She was grateful that, after her day-long rest, her middle no longer felt like an overfilled wineskin. The blood had been absorbed by her body. She stood, feeling stronger and refreshed, then crossed the room and opened her wardrobe.

Blue tonight, I think.

She settled on a dark blue dress and tunic from her collection, as well as one of her clean white aprons. *Got to look my best.* She changed before checking her teeth and face. Over time she had learned to do this by touch. She checked her hair and tied it back out of the way in a ponytail, keeping her fringe from being too much in the way. Satisfied, she wrapped a hooded cloak around her shoulders and made to head downstairs.

Then she stopped and shook her head with a smile.

ALYSSA

Glasses. Every time.

She picked them up from her dresser and pulled them on, adjusting them over her nose. She peered at the nearby mirror, where she observed a pair of glasses hovering in mid-air over a dress with nobody in it.

At least I'll always know if my face is clean or not.

Satisfied she was at last ready, she headed for her door. Then she paused again, her hand halfway to the handle, taking a breath.

No Vlad, no need to drink blood, no Craving. Maybe tonight will be a normal night.

She opened her door and stepped out into the cold winter night.

✝ ✝ ✝

Alyssa arrived at the Elk's Horn in quick time. Entering via the back kitchen door, she hung her cloak on the nearby hook. Then she turned to be immediately met by the tavern's premier bar mistress, Gretna.

"Alyssa," Gretna said in the low menacing growl of her race, looking up and giving Alyssa a critical stare. "What have I told you about your dress sense?"

"Ah." Alyssa found herself fidgeting under the dwarf's authoritative emerald eyes, her own gaze dropping and a hand moving to her glasses. "I have good taste?" she ventured without confidence, adding a hopeful smile as she dared to glance at her employer.

Gretna's deadpan expression stared back, and Alyssa immediately dropped her gaze again.

"No," Gretna stated bluntly. "I said your dress sense needs to emphasise more." One hand motioned to Alyssa in a circle. "Grakin's name, girl, don't people tell you how attractive you are? Don't you want to show 'it' off?"

"Ah…well." Alyssa avoided Gretna's glare. "Yes, but… you know."

"Alyssa." The dwarf's hands moved to her hips, one hand uncomfortably close to her family heirloom: a rather brutal hand hammer that was slid through the belt around her waist. "You've the best arse out of all the girlies here. Next time, wear something that emphasises that! It's good for business."

Alyssa's eyes widened. Even after working for so long in the Elk's Horn, she had never managed to get used to how direct Gretna was.

Gretna pointed an authoritative finger. "Remember next time."

"Yes, Gretna," she agreed, as the dwarf marched off toward the dining area, grabbing an apron off a hook as she went.

"And emphasise them breasts of yours as well!" Gretna yelled over her shoulder, her brown hair swinging in the braided ponytail she had made it up into, almost clipping one of the other girls. "Buy a corset!" The kitchen door slammed as she made her exit.

Alyssa felt like a person could cook eggs on her cheeks.

The other barmaids who happened to be in the kitchen at the time were looking at Alyssa, having had the good sense to stay quiet as Alyssa was both complimented and berated in the same breath. Some of them were regarding her with a certain jealousy, particularly the dwarves; others with shared embarrassment, whilst a few, predominantly the elves, were trying to check whether the dwarf's statement was true.

ALYSSA

Alyssa, cheeks still burning, found herself backing into the wall and hugging her chest, one hand self-consciously pushing her glasses up.

"Gretna's right."

It was Sarah who spoke, one of the tall, skinny elven barmaids from southern Argon, breaking the silence in the room. The audience as a whole immediately shifted their view to Sarah with collective eyebrows raised.

"Ah, not that I've been looking!" babbled Sarah, who suddenly found the board of vegetables needing chopped much more fascinating. Alyssa quickly slipped out and into the relative safety of the dining area by the same door Gretna had stormed through moments ago.

The Elk's Horn had an extensive dining area, with long tables and attendant benches or chairs sitting by, as well as cosy smaller private tables in alcoves around the side. It had rustic, varnished wooden floorboards and thick stylised wooden pillars stretching to the ceiling. Chandeliers of blackened metal provided candlelight to the whole area.

Customers sat, ate, drank, and talked all around the floor in small groups; there was a wide variety in tonight. Couples on dates, mostly elven, enjoying quieter drinks in the secluded corners. Groups of human and dwarf workmen slumped by the larger benches, drinking away a hard day's labour in the cold. Other groups of out-of-work men and women of many races were scattered across the area.

She found that only she and Gretna were out on the floor. Not wanting another berating in front of the customers, she immediately started doing her rounds, taking orders for drinks.

At least nothing worse can happen whilst I'm here.

✝ ✝ ✝

"Thanks for your time."

Victoria reached across to shake hands with Constable Shane, then with Constable Davin.

"Happy to help," replied Shane.

"Pleasure," said Davin.

"And good luck with that promotion." Victoria nodded to Davin. "That was excellent deduction. I hope you pass the exam."

"Thank you," said Davin, smiling self-consciously as the other constable smirked and shook his head.

The two constables collected their helmets before standing and saluting.

Victoria watched the two of them go from the other side of the interrogation room table. "Stop rolling your eyes, Malak."

"What?"

"I saw you do it." She scowled over at her colleague, who was leaning on the wall in the corner. "You always do that when I mention my militia service."

"Maybe because you *always* mention your militia service," her colleague shot back.

"I was wishing the kid well," Victoria protested, motioning to the open door through which the constables had made their departure. "Besides, let's hope he has better luck than us." She stood and started to collect the papers on the table together. "So, let's recap," she said as she started to pack the reports into a leather bag. "The spikes are dangerous, and they've been logged with the city council to be removed. Death is marked as suspicious, but nobody seems to be doing anything further about it now because we've got the case. Death Warden's report says…" She stopped her packing for a moment and checked the Death Warden's official parchment. "…almost exactly the same as the Corpse Wardens." She shoved the paper into the bag.

"And our trip to the scene of the incident," she let out a sigh, clipping the bag closed, "yielded no additional clues, though it did give you…" she nodded at Malak, "…a chance to learn a little more about using the right terms in detective work."

"We 'walked the scene.'" Malak nodded at his own remark. "I'm getting better."

Victoria sighed again. "I've got nothing. This has 'inconclusive' written all over it."

They left the room, thanking the militia sergeant on duty and leaving the watch house via its main entrance. Descending the stone steps that led down to the street level, past a couple of militia men struggling with a suspect, Victoria looked up into the quickly darkening sky. Clouds slid across the gloom. "And it was such a nice day," she said to herself.

Malak hummed as he walked beside her. "Snow again." He didn't hide his eye-rolling this time. "Your weather is terrible."

Victoria snorted. "Says the Tornarian? Sure, it's just as bad up north with you lot."

"I'll have you know we occasionally see this giant ball of light in the sky." Malak was puffing out his chest. "It's called 'the sun.'"

"And I'll have *you* know, you snarky git," Victoria replied, with a certain relish, "that we have that too." She pointed to a part

of the sky off in the distance, finding a cloud in the way. "It's…
behind that cloud."

They both regarded the cloud as they stood at the bottom of
the steps.

"Just give it a minute," said Victoria. They both paused for a
moment before smirking.

"Good comeback," Malak teased.

"Oh, shut up. It's nearly dark anyways."

"I'm hungry," grumbled Malak next, as they crossed the
road and clambered up into the coach for the third time that day.

"Back home, Harcan," Victoria ordered, ignoring Malak's
despair and thumping the backboard of the coach. The crack of a
whip could be heard as their driver set off.

"Aren't you?" Malak asked Victoria.

"Hungry?" Victoria shrugged, broken out of her contemplations as she read the papers they'd left in the coach. "Not really."

"Balls!" scoffed Malak with palpable disbelief. "I bet you
never even had a proper breakfast, did you?"

"I'll be fine," she said sternly. "Yes, I didn't have breakfast
but…" Unfortunately, it was at that moment that her stomach
decided to rather vocally disagree with her, emitting a low grum-
ble. It made Victoria flinch sharply, her mask of discipline slipping for a second. A smirk broke out over Malak's face.

"Your gut says otherwise," he said.

Victoria sighed, a hand going to her stomach. "Fine." She
folded her arms. "Where do you want to go?"

"Hanged Man?" he asked.

"I'm not desperate," she assured him. "We can afford to go
to a tavern, not a hole in the ground."

"Fine, what about the Broken Dreams? It's close."

"They don't serve food." Victoria made a face. "They say it's food but it isn't."

Malak rolled his eyes yet again.

The coach continued on its way. Outside, the world became much darker, night closing in fast. Malak kept watch as Victoria sat, tapping her chin, in deep thought.

"There must be somewhere we can grab a bite to eat," Malak mused.

Victoria's stomach grumbled, making her flinch again. "Oh shut up," she muttered.

"What?" asked Malak, momentary distracted.

"I wasn't talking to you."

Malak suddenly banged the inside front board of the coach with his fist. "Hold up, Harcan!" he shouted. The driver brought the coach shuddering to a halt.

Malak beckoned to Victoria. She leaned over to look past him, out of the window of the carriage. He was pointing across the street.

"What about that place?"

Sure enough, across from where they had stopped was a tavern. It was a large one, with clean shuttered windows set in walls of modern red brick. Shadows moved behind the well-lit windows.

She nodded her reluctant acceptance. "All right then, might be promising."

They had the coachman bring them round the front to drop them off. They were not too far from their work place, so Victoria bade Harcan return there.

"We'll walk back later," she assured him. The coach lurched off into the night, the darkness now having fully closed in during their short journey.

Victoria wrapped her all-weather cloak around her; there was still a biting cold in the air, and she beheld the sign that hung from the tavern's entrance. It seemed this place even had its own motto.

The Elk's Horn, read the sign. *Always fine food and fine company.*

"Heck with it," she said to Malak. "Maybe I am hungry after all."

✝ ✝ ✝

Alyssa cleared the elf couple's plates, smiling sweetly and being rewarded with a nod from both of them. Like all their kind, they had sharp features: high cheek bones and pointed ears, with eyes of ice blue and jade.

I like elves. Always so polite.

James was still to arrive.

It's early yet, she reminded herself.

Not so many customers were in tonight. It was halfway through the week, after all, and few enough could afford drinks during the week.

Gretna was just then seeing to a couple of newcomers. One was a woman, just in the process of hanging up a cloak. She was dressed in leggings and a tunic with a sword and pistol at her hip.

Probably a mercenary, Alyssa guessed.

The other, a man, had a more definite mercenary or soldier

ALYSSA

appearance to him. He was wearing armour and was festooned with weapons, right down to a nasty crossbow he had slung over his shoulder. They seemed to be ordering food.

Wonder who they are?

It was but a passing thought, however, for just at that moment a troupe of the regulars arrived. They were a squad of dwarfish miners, dusty tunics thick with dirt and with pick-axes slung over their shoulders. They slumped into a nearby corner, claiming their usual spot at one of the round tables. The head miner, a dwarf by the name of Lorcan, gave a wave to Gretna across the tavern; he made a series of gestures. The dwarf mistress waved back her assent.

Alyssa smiled; she recognised the sign language.

A good day's mining then.

Two orc Tax Reapers were just about to take their seats at another table, with marks of coin on their tabards and thick identical scimitars in scabbards slung across their backs.

A lot of weapon carriers in tonight.

She chose, rather tactfully, to approach the dwarves for their orders first of all.

Whilst all dwarves possessed the same directness that Gretna did (*"ye be a fine lass and no mistake. Some manling will count himself lucky the first time he snugs ye!"*) it was better them than the orcs. Orcs tended to have rather "busy" hands, coupled with high pain thresholds. Slapping them just didn't work.

Fortunately, all the miners seemed to be too exhausted to pass any comments designed to make Alyssa feel embarrassed, so she was able to take their orders without incident. She was back at the bar top just as Gretna arrived.

"Order for table four," Gretna informed Rodney, the lumbering orc barman with tiny black eyes, enormous jaw, and unexplained cooking skills. He screwed up his huge face, studying the slip of paper Gretna had reached across to him. "And the two orcs at table three want a couple of Gorrag's Draft," Gretna said next, addressing Alyssa.

Alyssa shuffled nervously, adjusting her glasses. "Do I…"

"…have to? Yes," Gretna snapped, interrupting her taller but younger colleague. "Besides, you're the quickest at dodging and they tend to complain when they get a hammer to the face." She patted her sheathed hammer with a smirk.

Alyssa nodded without confidence and moved around the bar, grabbing a couple of mugs and pouring the drinks from the Gorrag's barrel. She headed over to the orcs, leaving Rodney still translating Gretna's slip of paper and Gretna drumming her fingers.

Alyssa arrived at table three and immediately dodged a grab for her bottom from one of the orcs, rather expertly, she thought, as she managed to not even wobble the two mugs of the brown fluffy liquid she was carrying.

"Damn," grunted the offending orc.

"Told ye she was quick!" said his companion with a grin, paying for the two drinks.

As she left the table, a little voice interrupted her before she got to the bar again. "Hey, Alyssa."

Alyssa turned and found the short figure of Katy, smiling up at her. "You came!"

"I did." The other girl beamed. She glanced around at the busy tavern, her pigtails swinging. "So…how do I get in?"

"Probably best to get you introduced to Gretna first," Alyssa decided, nodding over toward the bar.

Katy straightened her dress, spreading out the creases on the light brown material. "Will this do?" she asked.

"Oh yes, it's pretty much the uniform here." Alyssa gave Katy's outfit an appraising nod. "I think she'll like the pigtails too." Alyssa stopped herself. "Just…Gretna can be a bit forward," she warned.

Katy seemed untroubled. "I worked at the Hanged Man, remember?"

"Oh yeah. That…that will definitely help." Relieved, Alyssa led Katy over to the bar top. Rodney had gone, and now Gretna was standing on a stool, wiping down a spillage and muttering dwarfish.

Alyssa nervously approached. "Gretna, this is Katy."

Gretna looked up from her work and nodded approvingly towards the girl. "Yes?"

Katy straightened herself, taking a breath. "I'd like a job, please?"

"Oh yes, of course, the ad I put out!" Gretna skillfully dismounted the stool, approaching the girl. "Ah, well, ye done any bar work before?"

"Yes, at the The Hanged Man."

Gretna's eyes widened. "Gograg-dan's name!" she exclaimed.

"That's what everyone says," Katy said, Alyssa nodding her agreement beside her.

"Ye would be keen to move on then?"

"Definitely," Katy enthusiastically confirmed.

Gretna gave the girl a once-over. She walked round her,

looking her up and down. Katy remained still, maintaining her smile.

"Very cute," the dwarf decided. Katy glanced away, pursing her lips with embarassment. "Alyssa, you go grab the legal documents."

"Will do!" Alyssa headed to the kitchen. Over Gretna's shoulder, she gave Katy a thumbs-up; Katy grinned.

☦ ☦ ☦

"You two friends?" asked Gretna, raising an eyebrow, as Alyssa disappeared through the kitchen door.

"Yes." Katy's face turned serious. "She saved my life."

Gretna's bushy eyebrows raised further. "Oh?"

"A big fat guy tried to…" Katy breathed, swallowing.

"It's all right, lass." Gretna drew close. "I was only being nosy, it's a dwarf thing. We have a racial need to know stuff."

"It's okay, I…I want to talk about it." Katy composed herself. "He was drunk; he tried to hurt me on Holt Street. Alyssa came by and rescued me."

"I know the type," Gretna agreed. "I'm glad one of my girls was in the area. A stroke of luck I'm sure, but a welcome one!"

"Got them!" Alyssa announced as she arrived back. She caught the seriousness of the situation almost immediately. "Everything okay?"

"Just hearing how you took care of Katy here." Gretna's expression was one of admiration. "What did you do?"

"I saw she was in trouble and…I knocked him out," Alyssa said, fidgeting with her glasses.

Gretna blinked in surprise. "*You* knocked him out?" she asked, raising both her eyebrows, hands moving to her hips.

"Yeah." Alyssa stumbled over her words. "I mean, it was hard, but yeah."

"Well done, girl!" Gretna said, moving to slap Alyssa rather hard on the arm. For effect, Alyssa winced. "You should get a medal for that! Can't stand nasty drunks. Anyways, take Katy over to the corner there and fill in the paperwork. Katy, consider yourself hired!"

"Oh, thank you!" Katy beamed.

"No hugs mind," warned Gretna. Katy stopped herself and quickly switched to a firm handshake.

"Thank you again."

Katy waved her hand vigorously until the feeling came back after the dwarf had let go.

Alyssa led Katy over to a nearby alcove with table and seats as Gretna returned to the kitchen.

Nearby, seated on the edge of her bench, Victoria Haldred leaned back again.

CHAPTER 5

OBSERVE AND REPORT

Malak returned to the table that Victoria and he had chosen. He gave the dwarf bar mistress respectable room as she brushed past him, then set a goblet of wine in front of his colleague and took a seat on the bench opposite Victoria.

"Just heard a very interesting conversation," she stated, formally.

"Oh?" he said, raising an eyebrow, his mug of ale halfway to his lips.

"Yes. Now, game face on and use your eyes, not your head. Peek over my left shoulder," she instructed. "Middle alcove along the back, blond girl in pigtails, other girl in glasses and blue dress."

Malak did just as Victoria ordered, setting his drink down and looking past her shoulder briefly, then returning to look at her. "Got them."

"The blond girl is called Katy." Victoria took a sip from her goblet. "The one with glasses is Alyssa. Katy has just been recruited here as a barmaid and Alyssa is filling out the parchment work."

"With you so far." Malak took a sip from his mug.

"Katy owes Alyssa a debt…because Alyssa saved Katy's life." Victoria leaned forward in a conspiratorial manner. "From a fat drunken guy, on Holt Street. Not far from…"

"Mounds Pathway," breathed Malak.

Victoria nodded approvingly. "Well done."

"You think it's the same fella?" asked Malak.

"I do."

He sat back, his expression thoughtful. "How'd she save her?"

"That's the interesting part." Victoria sipped from her drink again. "Apparently, by knocking him out."

Malak chuckled. "Front of the skull…"

Victoria nodded again. "Enough to knock him out. I like this, your memory for details is improving."

Malak made a face. "She doesn't appear to be the type, though, and aren't we searching for his murderer, instead of some girl who just roughed him up?"

"Fair point," Victoria conceded, "but his movements before his death are important. Working backwards, we can maybe figure out how he died."

Malak sipped his tankard thoughtfully. "Should we interview them?" he asked, studying his colleague.

"That's what I'm considering. Might reveal more about his final movements." She glanced over her shoulder, briefly. "Thing is…" She leaned forward again. "…how many young slips of girls do you know who can knock out a man the size of a bear?"

"I'm talking to one," Malak said, straight-faced.

Victoria leaned back, hiding her smile with her drink. "You pigging flirt," she chided him.

"Good one, though, wasn't it?"

"Yes, thank you, but I think we both know, with these hips, I'm no 'slip.'" Her expression sobered again. "Seriously, though, look that girl over."

Malak did just that, very briefly peering over Victoria's shoulder. He frowned. "Now hold on, you don't think?"

Victoria lifted a hand. "Lines of enquiry. I'm not saying it, but I'm not *not* saying it."

Malak gave his colleague a blank expression. "What?"

Victoria rolled her eyes. "What I mean to say, maybe she is, maybe she isn't. I'm not sure."

This time, Malak shook his head. "I don't...no, she doesn't look like one. And sure if I was a vampire, I'd not be working here. It's too public, lots of people. Surely someone would figure you out? Don't they live in castles and just eat peasants?"

"That's the stereotype, yes," Victoria agreed. "Certainly what Regorash did." She set her drink down and stroked her chin. "But what if this one is hiding," she ventured. "Trying to keep a low profile?"

"Playing a long game?"

"Maybe." Victoria shrugged. "I've no evidence, without talking to her. But, if she is a vampire, interviewing her would give things away. Same with interviewing the other girl. It would likely get back to Alyssa."

"You're not giving us a lot of options," Malak said "What do we do then? It's just a theory right now and with nothing backing it up."

Victoria held up her goblet, studying the red wine within. "What if we check Holt Street first?" She looked at him. "See if we can pick up anything?"

"Such as?"

"Signs of struggle?"

Malak moved his head from side to side, unconvinced. "Been a while, you really think you'd still find something?"

Victoria smiled ruefully. "I'd rather try searching there before I go anywhere near someone who might, and I mean might, be a vampire."

The two investigators returned to their drinks as they awaited their meals.

✝ ✝ ✝

Alyssa and Katy had selected a little alcove out of the way of the main hustle and bustle of the bar room, well to the rear of the building. Alyssa unrolled the registration of work document onto the table and set an inkwell and quill at the ready. "Okay?" she asked Katy.

The other girl nodded from the other side of the table.

"So first, what's your full name?"

Around them other barmaids wandered past, carrying trays or drinks. A fresh group of workmen arrived and took a seat in the far corner opposite where the dwarves had already set up camp. The smell of cooked food and fresh ale filled the air. Outside, the darkness of night was complete and the heat of the tavern was welcome.

"I know."

The counter-question stopped Alyssa for a moment. "…how to wait tables?" Alyssa suggested, though without confidence.

Katy responded with a warm smile, almost motherly in the way it seemed correcting. "No, Alyssa," she explained. "I mean, I know what you are."

Alyssa's eyes flickered. Katy stared.

Alyssa's breath caught in her throat. *No...she couldn't.* The answer hung in the air, pregnant with the need for action.

"It's okay. I'm a ghost seer," Katy began, in a low voice. "We can see the dead." The petite girl's eyes dropped to the table and she began to pick at the cracked surface. Alyssa looked on, her mouth slightly open, listening to Katy's confession. "I can see you plain as day." Her finger traced a deep grove in the wooden panels of the table. "You're not alive. No living creature has teeth that go all the way up into their skull and connect with your brain."

Katy met the other girl's pale and shocked expression. "I can see them. Like gazing through a dirty mirror. I see them," she cocked her head to one side, that smile returning, "and they say to me: 'I'm a vampire.'" Quite suddenly, Katy's hand was on Alyssa's. "But you don't need to worry," she went on. "I'll keep your secret. And, more importantly, I'll help you." She patted Alyssa's hand.

Alyssa blinked, her breathing slow. She swallowed before reacting. "What?" she finally managed.

"No vampire I've ever read about would so willingly step in to help someone, as you helped me." Katy's voice broke and dropped as she spoke. "And you didn't step in just to feed on that guy. You did it to help me."

Alyssa bit her lip. "You…" she began, but Katy interrupted.

"…Saw it all, yes." Katy shrugged. "I couldn't help it, I'd never actually seen it before. I've seen vampire drawings before but just not real and close up. It's…" Katy made an apologetic face. "…kind of a morbid fascination for me."

Alyssa's hand, the one holding her inked quill, was shaking now. A small pool of ink had built up where she was on the parchment.

Katy gently removed the quill and set it back in its inkwell. "I know this is a lot to take in."

"Ye think?" Alyssa said out loud, before ducking her head, fearing she'd spoken too loudly. She looked around, but no one seemed to notice.

"At least you never have to admit to being a vampire to me?" Katy suggested.

Alyssa's mouth opened and closed a few times before she replied. "That…that wasn't really on the cards just yet, if I'm honest." Alyssa sat back, exhaling. "This is a lot to process," she concluded, after staring at the ceiling for a few considered moments.

"For both of us," Katy said.

"I knew one day, someone was bound to figure it out. Just…" she motioned to Katy "…not someone I'd just met, no offence."

"That's okay." Katy leaned forward, whispering now. "But I'm nice, really I am. And I'm telling the truth. I want to help."

"I wish I believed you," Alyssa said, "you *seem* nice. But vampires don't have a great reputation. I mean, I don't consider myself an average vampire."

"You're *definitely* not."

"Thank you, but I still come with that warning. I know the

history. Even before Regorash, it's always been…" She trailed off with a prolonged sigh.

"…evil," Katy finished for her.

"Yes," Alyssa's answer was mournful, "so much…bad. Vampires are terrible. What is it the Council of Peace calls us? A confirmed threat to peace?"

Katy nodded slowly. "Yeah, 'fraid so."

"My only chance is to change back." She spread her arms in a gesture of defeat. "I don't see that happening."

Katy opened her mouth to answer but was interrupted as Gretna approached them.

"Right, you two, the rest of the parchment work can wait. I've just found out we've a couple of special guests here and I need you two on the floor to cover."

"What guests?" asked Alyssa, shakily bundling the paper and quill into her arms.

"Couple of Council of Peace Investigators."

Both Katy and Alyssa's eyes went wide. Alyssa found herself loudly gulping. "Council of Peace?" she spluttered.

"Yeah, they popped in for grub, but I'll not have my establishment found wanting!" declared Gretna, puffing her chest out. "They came in with the badges, so I'll not see them eat the usual rubbish, no no! I've got Rodney on the fires preparing the best stuff."

"Sorry," Katy interrupted, "maybe I don't know the history here, but, why?"

Gretna looked to Katy in shock, her eyes wide. "Why? Youngster, the outbreak of Peace, of course!" She waved her arms in an overly dramatic gesture, almost making Katy and Alyssa lean back out of range. "The Six Nations War would still be raging if the Council of Peace hadn't done such fine work in bringing all the knuckleheaded morons together and forcing them to a treaty! My people would still be building forts and steam machines and Gorvator knows what else!" Gretna thrust her hands to her hips, glaring at both girls. "We'll show them the proper respect, we will! Let them know that this dwarf and all who serve under her will ever be in their debt!" She stared off into the corner of the tavern for a moment.

"Anyway," Gretna caught herself, "long story short, you two do the floors. The other girls are giving Rodney a hand putting the finishing touches to the grub we're giving them, 'nough said." Gretna spun on her heel and marched off.

Katy and Alyssa didn't say anything for a moment, both staring after the dwarf. It was Katy who broke the silence. "I'm sorry, what just happened?"

"Gretna," Alyssa answered. "Gretna happened."

Katy raised one eyebrow.

"Yeah, get used to it," Alyssa told her.

✝ ✝ ✝

Hunched over, Smithy watched the two girls stand from the table, both chatting. He grimaced.

"Here," said Davidson as he approached the table the workmen had taken. "On the house, mate." A tankard was dropped down in front of Smithy, but he hardly noticed.

"Thank you," Davidson said sarcastically as he took a seat with the other men at the table, big hands grasping for the tankard he had gotten himself. "What you looking at anyway, Smithy?"

"The girl over there," he growled.

Morris chuckled from beside Davidson. "She's not your type, mate," he said in his high-pitched voice. "Wouldn't go for a fella like you."

"Nah, not like that." Smithy twisted round on his stool and pulled open his coat. Inside, the two men opposite could see the handle of a knife.

"Keep that covered up!" hissed Davidson, leaning close. "Gretna'll have your guts!"

"Don't be daft, I'd not pull it here."

"What you up to, Smithy?" asked Morris, leaning in like his friend. "You gonna rob her?"

"Yeah, I am," Smithy said with a smirk. "Pretty young thing is always dressed so fancy. She'll have coin and no mistake."

"You're a nasty piece of work, you know that?" Morris said, leaning back and shaking his head. Davidson did the same after a moment. Smithy continued to grin before turning on his stool to continue his observation.

Behind him, Morris whispered to Davidson, "Remind me why we're friends with him again?"

✝ ✝ ✝

"I'll need a clear head to think this through," Victoria said at length, having finished her goblet. She peered into the cup before setting it to one side. "Next drink you get me is going to be clear water. No alcohol," she instructed. "What did you order me, meal-wise?"

"Your usual, just a steak sandwich," Malak told her.

"Happy days."

Victoria could see a large orc approaching them from the bar. "Speaking of which," she nodded over to the tray that the orc was carrying, "that was quick."

Victoria didn't catch what exactly was on the tray as the orc set it on the tables behind them. It was only when the orc picked up the plate and set it before them that both she and Malak got a good look at what was arrayed upon it.

"That…" began Malak, the first to speak after a polite pause. "…is one hell of a steak."

Victoria nodded. It was an extensive cut of prime steak, freshly cooked. "Is this right?" she asked tentatively, looking up at the towering orc with a raised eyebrow. "I think my colleague ordered me the steak sandwich, not the *whole* cow."

The orc shrugged his huge shoulders. "That's what I was given," he said, forming the words slowly. "The miss said, 'get the good stuff for them, you great oaf, and stop staring down my top'. Said that we ought to reward them who serves the Council of Peace for their fine work in keeping the peace, 'cause we is dead grateful."

Victoria frowned. "Well, ah." She found herself lost for words. "Please convey our…thanks."

The orc nodded and wandered off, leaving Victoria staring at her breakfast, lunch and tea rolled into one.

"I've never seen that expression before." Malak was studying his colleague.

"That's because this is my scared expression, Malak," replied Victoria, blinking at the steaming pile of food in front of her that was taking up most of the large plate it sat on.

"Proper scared of that, aren't you?" Malak nodded toward the plate.

Victoria nodded slowly. "Oh Gods, yes."

Victoria studied the meal as the orc moved off back to the kitchen.

"What do we do?" asked Malak.

"Can't send it back," Victoria said. "I mean, if this is a gift. It would be downright rude to refuse, and this is expensive stuff." Victoria bit her bottom lip.

"You think you can finish it?"

"Heck no," Victoria was happy to admit. "I doubt even a fey could finish this, and you know what those weirdos are like."

"Don't worry," Malak began, his expression thoughtful. "I mean, I didn't order much, so I'm sure I can give you a hand with…"

His encouragement was cut short when a plate of cooked goose was set in front of him with a dull thud, complete with extra potatoes and vegetables.

Now they both stared with mute shock.

"We're just proper blessed tonight, aren't we?" Malak remarked.

With a distinct lack of confidence, Victoria picked up her knife and fork.

"Okay, ah." She looked across at Malak, then down at her meal again. "Good luck, I guess."

ALYSSA

"...and that's how much we charge for the Gorrag's Draft," Alyssa said.

"Got it," Katy said.

Having schooled Katy in the costs of the various drinks, Alyssa again found her eyes drawn to the area where the two Council of Peace investigators were huddled, working their way through the feast Gretna had bestowed on them.

"Alyssa?" Katy's voice interrupted Alyssa's troubled thoughts.

"Uh?"

"You're worrying too much," the other girl suggested.

"No," Alyssa said. "I think...I think I'm worrying the right amount. Maybe not enough."

"They're just here for food," Katy assured her. "If they were hunting for you surely they would have come up to you already."

Alyssa sighed. "I suppose."

Katy took Alyssa's hand. "It's okay; stop fretting. You've got lots more to show me, I'm sure."

Alyssa nodded. "I'll show you where the latrines are."

"Yeah." Katy made a face, and Alyssa tittered.

"Maybe leave that till the end. I'll show you the barrels instead."

They made for the other end of the bar top. Two of the other barmaids, Sarah and another girl Alyssa recognised, Hayley, were propping up the bar.

"Fiver on the guy," said the elf, Sarah, as Alyssa and Katy drew near.

"Six on the woman," replied Hayley, the young dwarf, balancing on her stool.

"What you girls talking about?" asked Alyssa.

"Bets on which of the Council of Peace people finishes their plate."

Alyssa smiled. "No bet." They all shared a laugh.

"I don't think you'll have much to worry about from those two," Katy whispered, as they moved behind the bar.

"Why?"

"That amount of food." Katy shook her head. "I'll be surprised if they even remember who they are by the time they're finished."

✝ ✝ ✝

"You are never choosing the tavern again. Ever!" said Victoria.

It didn't take long for a coach to be summoned for the two of them. It was one with cushions for both of them to rest their exhausted bodies on. Victoria steadied herself on the railing on the inside of the coach as it rattled through the night.

"Point taken," Malak managed. He was doing the same, trying to roll with the potholes.

"I've never eaten so much in my whole life," gasped Victoria, her other hand on her stomach. "So glad we got a coach. I don't think I could have walked anywhere quickly."

"Same here," replied Malak. "That was a bloody huge bird."

"I think mine was *the* cow."

"You know what I think?" he said next.

"What?"

"We need to stop doing such a great job," he said with a cheeky smile. "'Cause if this is the reward…"

"Very funny." Victoria leaned back, trying to get comfortable.

"Do you think they were maybe trying to kill us? I mean with the food."

Malak chuckled. "No, but they very nearly did."

"Don't speak too soon," Victoria warned him. She rubbed her head. "Gods, my head is fried. Couldn't wait to get out of there and…" She stopped herself. "Damn it!"

"What?"

"The girls." She looked over at him. "The suspects. We didn't interview them."

"I thought we'd decided not to?"

"I know but…" Victoria let out an exasperated breath. "When two prime witnesses who saw the recently deceased potentially minutes before he died just pop up, you don't just…" She trailed off, grimacing. "Okay, maybe you're right; they were *literally* trying to kill us with food."

Malak shook his head, sniggering.

"Right," Victoria decided, "we pick this up first thing tomorrow. I'll complete my daily report, then we go check out the crime scene again, and after, we track those two down."

"Agreed."

"Elk's Horn should be registered," Victoria went on, "so they'll have an up-to-date list of staff. We can cross-reference names and confirm when which staff are on which rota."

"So, what you're saying is, your brain isn't actually that fried."

"I'm talking fast to try and distract myself enough so I don't throw up," Victoria quickly explained, before her stomach interrupted them with a loud, pained groan. "I swear," she said with a grimace, "it honestly feels like the cow is trying to work its way back up my throat."

Malak snorted, and even Victoria smiled at the absurd situation she and her partner found themselves in.

"I learned one thing, though," Victoria admitted, glancing out the coach window as the night time lanterns flashed past.

"What's that?"

"Skipping breakfast is a bad idea."

✝ ✝ ✝

Alyssa and Katy watched out of the tavern's front shutter windows as the coach disappeared into the night. Only when it was completely gone did they both breathe a sigh of relief.

"I kind of feel sorry for them," said Katy, as she turned to Alyssa. "They didn't look well."

"They gone then?" Gretna approached the girls with her arms crossed.

"Yes," Alyssa said. She gave Gretna a relieved smile; the dwarf tavern mistress replied with a raised eyebrow. "They just make me nervous," Alyssa explained.

"Oh, don't be daft," replied the dwarf, though not with malice. "They're the good guys, you trust me on that! My husband's got big respect for them, and so do I! You weren't here at the time, but a while back their lot did a good deed for this tavern."

"I was meaning to ask, what was that…deed?" Katy enquired, carefully.

"Bunch of smugglers were trying to shift black powder explosives through this very tavern!" declared the dwarf mistress. She wagged a finger. "A true professional fella by the name of Maldor came in. Caught them red-handed, arrested them and got them all out, without bother. Made sure it was all done real professional. Almost dwarf level of efficiency!"

"That's high praise," Alyssa put in.

"It is indeed!" agreed Gretna. "Now," she declared, "to other matters." Gretna smiled slyly, as the fox smiles before the chicken coop.

"Oh." The dawn of realisation crept over Alyssa's face. "Oh dear."

"Tomorrow night, corset and something tight," ordered the dwarf, before turning on her heel and marching back into the kitchen.

Katy raised an eyebrow.

"Don't ask," said Alyssa.

Just then the tavern's door swung open with a bang and a panting figure in a brown work cloak entered. All eyes turned.

"Am I too late?" gasped the figure as he pulled his hood back and looked around the dining room.

Alyssa's face lit up. "James!" she squealed, before leaping from her chair and grabbing him in a bear hug. She stopped herself rather abruptly. *I'm an idiot.* She let him go, blushing fiercely. "Ah, sorry," she said, fixing her glasses. "I mean, so glad you could make it."

"My pleasure," replied James, blinking in surprise. Katy looked from one to the other with a puzzled expression.

"Oh, sorry, Katy. This is James. James, this is Katy."

"Hello." The two of them shook hands.

"Hey," returned Katy. "Your boyfriend?"

Both James and Alyssa coughed at the same time before laughing nervously. Katy rolled her eyes. "Kids these days," she muttered with a smirk, before skipping off to the kitchen.

Alyssa smiled broadly and James had the sense to melt before it.

"So glad you could make it," she said, feeling her cheeks still burning.

"Glad I could come," he replied, his fluster leaving him. "Sorry I wasn't here earlier. Work was busy today."

I'm not sorry you arrived late, thought Alyssa. *You just missed me having several heart attacks!*

"It was busy here too," she settled on. "Ah, grab yourself a drink," she said, gesturing over to the bar. "I've just to clean up and then we can...talk."

☦ ☦ ☦

Smithy sneered, watching the young couple from his perch.

"Maybe next time, mate," Davidson advised as he passed by.

Smithy ignored him, pulling his coat around himself.

"Don't encourage him," Morris said, as they and the rest of the docklands workers pulled on their coats and prepared to leave.

Smithy, after a brief delay, joined his comrades. "I'll get her alone," he muttered himself, ignoring the looks of concern from the other men around him. "Somehow."

☦ ☦ ☦

A little while later the tavern was more or less cleared, the stragglers taking the hint and leaving. Alyssa asked for some time with James, which Gretna duly agreed to. With a reminder of her obligations for the next night, of course (*"No excuses!"*).

ALYSSA

At last, she sat down opposite him with a drink of freshwater, he with a mug of cider. He smiled at her.

"Hey," she said, flashing him a smile in return.

He beamed, grinning broadly. "Hey."

They sat in silence, at least as silent as a tavern at clear-up time can be.

I get the feeling he's not entirely sure how to proceed, thought Alyssa. *And neither am I.*

Across the table wasn't going to work, she decided, so she looked around before moving to sit beside him on the bench. He blinked.

"It's okay, James," she assured him. "I'm just going to kiss you."

He chuckled. "I think I can agree with that," he managed.

She beckoned him to lean forward. He, a little unsure, complied. He was rewarded with a kiss on the lips. His breathing was quick, and she could practically feel his heart beating. She leaned back. "Are we okay?" she asked with a sly smile, enjoying once again being the more experienced one of the relationship.

"Oh yeah," he said, with a grin. They kissed again, much longer this time.

She let him be a little more confident. His tongue…

"Ouch!"

James flinched back, a hand going to his lips.

"Are you okay?" Alyssa asked.

James had stuck his tongue out, and was feeling it with his fingers. "It's okay," he smacked his lips, "think I just got nipped by one of your teeth."

Alyssa's heart stopped; her eyes widened.

She felt it now. A single drop of blood on her tongue, a single drop of…elixir.

"You've really sharp teeth, I think maybe my tongue…"

Alyssa's heart started hammering in her chest. She stared at him, feeling her eyes widen with fright.

Not here. Not now. Not like this!

"Alyssa?"

No, no don't!

She shut her eyes, lowering her head and feeling one hand grip the side of the table.

"Seizure?"

She nodded with difficulty at his question, swallowing and squeezing her eyes as tight as she could. She felt tears nipping at the edges of her eyelids. She shook, her knuckles becoming white under the strain. One hand gripped the table, the other balled in a fist by her side.

I have already fed. I have already fed. I have already fed.

"It'll be all right." James's hand was on her shoulder. His hand…skin…so close. She felt them, nipping at the inside of her mouth. Her teeth, growing, threatening to push out.

I have already fed. I have already fed. I have already fed.

She gritted her teeth, physically pushing the blade-like points back into her jaw.

I have already fed!

Stop!

She exhaled and slumped forward, gasping for air.

"It's okay, it's okay."

James's voice came, and his hands rubbed her back as she remained slumped over, facing him. Her breathing slowed. She flexed her hands, relieving the tension, letting go of the edge of the table. She was aware that now the edge of the solid wood had four new grooves where her hands had gripped so hard.

Eventually she rose, sitting up straight again. She wiped her face. "That's twice now," she said out loud, looking to him, still feeling herself trembling. "I'm so sorry."

"It's fine, please."

They held hands, he reaching for her. She recoiled, but then let his touch calm her. Slowly, she blinked away the tension and stress.

He leaned forward and to her surprise, Alyssa found herself kissing him again. She did not back away, but she did not let him in as far. They kissed on the lips, for long moments. It became comforting and distracting. Safer.

When they did break it off, she found his eyes closed and a very goofy grin plastered over his face.

You poor sap, she thought. *How many times is that going to happen?*

Alyssa reluctantly had to return to helping with the cleanup. She and Katy finished not long after. James waited patiently by the bar, with a complimentary drink of water. Gretna had given her approval (*"Aye, he'll do."*), so it was safe enough for him.

Alyssa arranged with Katy to help her sort her corset for the next night. "I'll get one, somehow, and can you help me attach it?"

Katy had agreed. "Be careful," she advised. "There are a lot of designs, just get one that isn't too much."

All was closed off and packed away, the few remaining kitchen girls of the tavern slipping away one by one through the back door. It was Gretna who made the discovery. "Girls?" Gretna called over to the youngsters assembled by the door.

Katy, James, and Alyssa looked over. Gretna was frowning as she nodded over at a table. "I think one of those Council people left their crossbow behind."

CHAPTER 6

CASE REVIEW

There, lying propped by a bench, was indeed a crossbow.
A long blocky-looking thing with a metal box attached
underneath it and notches carved down one side.

"They'll not be back tonight," said Gretna, retrieving the
crossbow and looking it over. "If they do come back at all, it'll
be tomorrow."

She's right, thought Alyssa.

Gretna headed over to the bar, tutting about "sad human
copies" and "not dwarfish enough" as she carried the crossbow
like a struggling toddler.

Alyssa smiled nervously.

"Nothing to worry about," Katy assured Alyssa.

Gretna looked up from behind the bar as she secured the
crossbow. "Wouldn't want the good guys making you nervous!"
she said with a touch of sarcasm.

Thank goodness you don't know the truth, Alyssa thought.

Katy and Alyssa shared a hug, then Katy bid both Alyssa

and James farewell.

Alyssa and James found their arms linking as they trudged off toward Alyssa's home through the cold, snowy streets. Above them, a full moon glinted down. "I never like that moon," James said.

"Oh? Why not?" Alyssa asked.

"It brings out the strange things in this world."

Alyssa chuckled.

"What?" asked James.

Alyssa shook her head, hiding the glint of tears in her eye. "You have no idea…" she breathed.

☥   ☥   ☥

Alyssa lay gazing up at her ceiling, Mr Rabbit cuddled in her arms and a bright smile on her face. It had been a wonderfully slow walk home with James. They talked at length. Work, life, butterflies, how cold it was, even about glasses; she discovered, to her delight, that he wore glasses as well, though only for fine detailed engineering work. He talked about daytime; she listened intently, reminding herself of what a wonderful thing the rising sun was. She talked about clothes; he was polite enough to listen, nodding his head at all the right parts and smiling sweetly.

All very mundane, but it had felt so nice to her. For her, mundane was appreciated. She would take a boring conversation about the weather any time over having to run over roofs or hide from sunlight. He'd walked with her all the way home. As a reward, she'd let him be the bold one and lean in for the kiss. He was getting more confident.

It had erased, almost, what had happened in the tavern. She tightened her grip on Mr Rabbit as that memory paraded itself before her mind's eye. Her tongue licked at her teeth.

Too close. Too close again.

She took a breath.

A fair night. Eventually. As long as I don't see those investigators again and don't cut James again.

She frowned.

Corset. Think I'll just be writing off tomorrow night from the get-go.

She closed her eyes, doing her best to think only of James, and entered her dream state.

☩   ☩   ☩

The shadow lowered itself to the ground again, trailing wisps of inky darkness as it moved.

"We must hurry, Great Leader," the golden-faced man warned from the alleyway. "The morning…"

"Is no threat to me," answered the shadow, in a low growl.

It solidified into the shape of a cloaked and hooded man once again. His hood craned up at the window of Alyssa's house. "Make haste with our plans," the figure commanded.

The golden-faced man bowed. "I shall, Director of Fate."

Both individuals studied the bedroom window above them. "Regorash chose poorly," the hooded figure grumbled, "but his mistake is our opportunity."

He looked at last to his partner. "So I will it," he ordered, "so shall it be."

ALYSSA

The golden-faced man bowed again as his master passed him by. "I shall," he confirmed.

They both disappeared into the night, in different directions.

✝ ✝ ✝

Victoria waved her hand until the feeling came back.

She had made it back to her home without decorating any of the streets of Larrick City with steak and potatoes. Good going, considering the coach driver seemed to have some perverted glee in running over every pothole in the road.

She had gotten home and slept for a *long* time.

She was now back in her office. She ran a hand through her hair, checking that her ponytail was still secured. Breathing out, she signed her name on the parchment's most recent update.

At this point, Malak arrived. He was downcast as he closed the door behind him. "Morning," he grumbled. He was dressed in his usual armour plate.

"Morning," she replied. "Sleep well?"

"Oh yeah," he said, sheepishly taking a seat by the wall. "Sleep was fine."

"Not the reply I was expecting. I'd an awful night when I finally rolled into bed. Oh." She groaned, feeling her stomach. "I'm still recovering. I felt like a pig fattened for slaughter."

When Malak didn't say anything more, Victoria looked over at him as he took his usual seat. His eyes were down, and his demeanour distracted. He seemed almost diminished. He was rubbing his forehead.

She frowned at her colleague. "What did you do?" she asked tentatively.

He shuffled in his seat uneasily. "You know my K-12?"

"Hard not to."

He paused, flinching. "I left the bloody thing at the tavern."

Victoria lifted her hand to her forehead. "Hell's depths," she breathed.

"I just forgot." He spread his arms in a gesture of apology.

"I can understand why," she said. "Don't think I need to rhyme off anything about equipment care, not like we wanted to stick around. Thing is…" She gave him a look. "…that means we have to go back more publicly than I would like."

He nodded gravely.

"Well, anyway," she said, reaching for a mug she had set beside her. "Good news is the daily report's done." She sipped at the cooling coffee within.

Malak frowned. "Conclusions?" he asked.

She shook her head. "Don't worry. I put 'inconclusive'. Not enough evidence."

"Great. The last thing you need is Horna jumping on anything."

There came a knock at the door.

"Come in," Victoria said, with a hint of boredom.

"Begging your pardon, miss." One of the Council of Peace guards spoke, poking his head through the door. It was one of the old ex-Argon legionnaires that the council employed, an older man by the name of Garlow, short of height and hair, with a podgy, grizzled face. "But the Overseer wants to see you. He's requesting progress on the vampire investigation."

Victoria frowned. "That's odd." She looked at Malak. "He doesn't normally ask for progress reports. Especially this early."

Malak shrugged, as did Garlow. Victoria picked up the pile of papers beside her, shuffling them into a roll of parchment. "All right. Back in a sec," she said to Malak. She paused to let Garlow leave the room before speaking again to Malak in a whisper. "And summon a coach. We'll go collect your crossbow shortly."

Malak mouthed "thank you."

✝ ✝ ✝

The Overseer's sanctum was in its own miniature keep at the far end of the Council of Peace compound. It was a circular keep, an ex-Argon military cannon fort dotted with banners and flags denoting various merchant families and departments that worked within; it was here that the various other Overseers had their headquarters.

"You all right?" asked Garlow as the two of them marched in step beside each other toward the keep from the inner archway.

"What do you mean?"

"You look like hell," the guardsman observed.

Victoria scowled at her escort. "Thanks, Garlow. What every girl wants to hear."

"Well, you do," the guardsman said, without apology. "You feeling okay?"

"Visited the Elk's Horn last night and they tried to kill us with kindness," she explained. "Upgraded the food we ordered from a snack to a pigging feast."

"Oh right." The former legionnaire chuckled. "Too much food?"

"Gods yes," Victoria admitted.

"They like us there."

"Oh?"

"Oh yes. Kane Maldor's teams did some work there a while back," Garlow explained, a hint of admiration in his voice. "Gretna, the bar mistress there, she always takes care of any Council of Peace people."

"We should have talked to you before we went," Victoria said.

They approached the fort, slowing their pace.

"Aye, it's a shame isn't it?" Garlow was craning up at the bunting strung from the building.

"The fort?"

"Aye." Garlow shook his head. "It just doesn't seem right, all those banners. She was a finer lady, bestowed with cannons."

Victoria allowed Garlow a small smile. "I suppose."

She climbed the great stone steps at the entrance of the keep. Two formidable Halnas-born orc mercenaries guarded the inner and outer doors, dressed in shirts of black ringmail and leather plate, glaring at them as they approached.

"Papers," they growled.

Garlow ensured both of them passed through the security swiftly. The orc grimaces were replaced with smiles once they had cleared security with their metal badges. Not that that was a major improvement; there was little difference between an orc smile and an orc grimace.

Inside the circular, marble-floored entrance hall, various doorways led off into the many political kingdoms within the expansive keep. Guards stood or sat at each door according to departmental whims; humans, orcs and ogres, all of them bored.

ALYSSA

They were flamboyantly dressed for the most part in bright colours, most clashing badly with the weapons they carried. Signs read Racial Relations Department (RDD), Secret Operations Department (SOD), Economics Department (E department) and so on.

Garlow led Victoria to the third door on the left, which was unguarded.

The personal heraldry of Horna Gladwell was displayed above the door frame, its bronze form dominating: two rampant lions facing outwards, whilst at the centre, a dragon with wings raised leapt out from the middle, mouth agape. The casting was disturbingly realistic, right down to the sharpness of the fangs and the rough-looking scales. Its eyes were two ruby-red gems, polished clear. Above the imposing door frame, the sign "Investigations Department (ID)" was carved in mundane script on a wooden panel.

Victoria felt her hand go to where her rapier should be. Garlow pushed open the door without comment or concern.

At the end of the short stone-clad corridor beyond the door, they came to a small table where a short worried elf sat up with a start. "Hello, Victoria," she said in a childish voice, sounding even younger than she appeared. She studied Victoria for a moment. "You alright?"

"This is going to be a feature of today," Victoria said. She heard Garlow snort with laughter behind her.

"No, Glynis," she replied, carefully. "I've just eaten a bit too much last night."

"Oh right. You're not feeling…"

"Not feeling the best, no. Still no joy with that voice of yours?"

Victoria asked in a vain attempt to redirect the conversation.

"No," Glynis said, disheartened, fidgeting with her blond locks. "One of the other attendants suggested whiskey."

"Really?"

"I declined." The elf woman chuckled. "I've no great wish to demonstrate just what a lightweight I am."

By this stage, Garlow had composed himself.

"You all right there, Garlow?" Victoria asked him, her face a blank mask.

"Aye...sorry, just..."

"I know, I know." She motioned to the double oakwood doors of the Overseer's office. "Just knock, let's get this over with, so I can go lie down somewhere."

Garlow knocked. There was a muted "Come" from beyond and Garlow pushed the doors open, allowing Victoria to enter.

Horna Gladwell's sanctum was a huge square affair. Dotted over the grey stone walls was all manner of military equipment and paintings depicting battles or individual soldiers. Here an Argon legion short sword, there a Trima tribal battle shield. A painting depicting the seventh battle of Murphy's Pass was on the left-hand wall, flanked by two Legion Long Lances in mint condition. bearkin two-handed blades, ogre battle axes, Darnhun bolt spitter repeater crossbows; the area would not have been out of place in a museum of warfare.

Horna sat at the far end, behind an extensive and exquisitely carved oak desk. Two tall candle holders cast as coiling dragons sat beside and behind him, whilst light to the vast room was pro vided by two huge bottle glass windows, edged in black steel. He had his head down as she entered, reading over a scroll.

"Victoria," he mused, not bothering to look up. "How nice of you to come."

"Sir," she said without enthusiasm, as the large doors behind her closed, sealing her in. "You wanted an update sir?" she asked, holding up her parchment.

A hand emerged from fine, black robes and beckoned for her to bring it over. Horna still did not look up from his work. She approached the desk, her footsteps echoing across the stone-tiled floor, and deliberately set her rolled-up parchment in front of him.

"Hmpt." He glanced from his hand to the scroll Victoria had set before him. At last, he raised his head. Two sharp evil eyes, dark brown and almost rat-like, regarded her above a small greying moustache and beneath a balding head.

Victoria glared down at him. "Anything else?" she asked, doing her best to ignore the cramp in her stomach.

"Perhaps one simple question," he said with a slightly crooked smile. He dropped his voice. "Is there a vampire on the loose, or isn't there?"

"The *current* report," Victoria began carefully, "suggests not enough evidence either way. I filed it inconclusive for now."

His face darkened. "Not good enough," he stated, pushing the parchment back across the table to her. "This is one report you cannot file under *that* heading."

She stiffened and leaned forward, hands on the table to look him in the eye. One hand moved the parchment back toward him. "Without enough evidence, I can't make a judgement I can stand by."

He didn't flinch, though there was at least some effort behind his eyes. "Regardless," he pushed the parchment back, "this comes from higher than me and definitely higher than you. We need a conclusive assessment."

"How can I?..." she began, but he cut her off with a wave of his hand.

"I am hearing excuses," he said, with palpable arrogance. "I need answers, not excuses. If you lack evidence, find more. This tasking is to be completed with a *definitive* conclusion. The final analysis is *not* to be inconclusive."

She picked up the parchment and nodded stiffly. "I'll do my best," she assured him.

"I'm sure you will," he replied, a smirk creeping across his face.

Victoria turned on her heel and strode from the room, with the demeanour of a royally pissed-off lioness, her ponytail flicking out behind her like an uncoiled whip.

She pushed open the heavy entrance doors with more force than necessary, startling both Garlow and Glynis as she exited. The doors swung closed behind her.

Glynis swallowed nervously. "I take it he didn't give you an answer you appreciated?" she chanced.

Victoria glared over. "No, not what I wanted to hear."

Glynis gave her a nervous smile. "We can but try."

Victoria composed herself before bidding the two of them farewell and beginning her march back to her office.

✝ ✝ ✝

Victoria and Malak quickly boarded a coach and made for the original crime scene, despite Malak's uncharacteristically whiny protests. He was rather concerned for his beloved crossbow.

"Look, one of your mates from the mercenary section said he's been over to the Elk's Horn." Victoria explained as the two of them made their way outside of the Council of Peace compound to the waiting carriage. Victoria had stopped by one of the mercenary checkpoints on her way back, on the off chance one of Malak's colleagues knew of the tavern. She'd spoken with one of Malak's friends, not wishing for him to get in trouble with his superiors. "It's safe and available to pick up any time."

"One of the boys? Ah no, Victoria, I'll be a laughing-stock now!"

"No pleasing you, is there?" Victoria grumbled as she boarded.

It was her intention to take a fresh perspective on the case. That proved to be more difficult than they expected.

They arrived to find the crime scene had changed drastically.

"That was quick," commented Malak as they came up to the suspected area. They were on top of the Mounds Pathway, looking down at where the dangerous spiked railings should have been. Instead, along each side of the path, the railings were gone, small holes in the ground the only indications that anything had been set there before.

"Very quick," Victoria said, frowning. "Nothing gets done this quickly. City council bureaucracy alone would have delayed this for weeks."

"Wonder why?" mused Malak.

Victoria regarded the scene, eyes scanning over the swift work that had evidently taken place. "Why indeed," she murmured.

"What made you think we'd find anything else here anyway?" Malak asked.

"It's not the scene itself," she said, turning to him. "I'm interested in what led to it."

She beckoned to him and he handed her the roll of parchments he had been carrying for her.

"Working backwards…" she began, unrolling her notes "…we find our drunk…ah…here." She pointed to a particular hole in the ground. "Bear with me, not sure that's the exact point, but it'll do."

In this area of the city, no fresh snow had fallen and what appeared like dried blood was visible on the ground nearby.

"He stumbled, or was pushed or thrown, down the slope and impaled himself on a spike. The stumble, let's assume for now…" She moved a little more to the edge of the mound they were on. "…may have been caused by the uneven ground, and the fact that he was weak with both drunkenness…" She cast Malak a look. "…and loss of blood."

"Here we go," muttered Malak.

"Question. Where did he come from?"

"Well…" Malak began, "…when a mummy and a daddy love each other very much…"

"He came from Holt Street," Victoria interrupted her colleague. "Or so our barmaids would have us believe. That's after one of them knocked him out, apparently."

Malak frowned. "You don't believe them?"

"Oh, I believe them, from overhearing their conversation,"

confirmed Victoria, her eyes finding the aforementioned Holt Street in the near distance. "I just don't think we've heard the whole story."

They headed away from the Mounds Pathway, down a gentle path toward Holt Street. It was not too long a walk; the Mounds Pathway was not long. Holt Street did not deserve the name; it was little more than a lane between buildings, an interconnecting route within the southern district. Alleys led off to one side or another, most into dead ends, all without lamplight poles. Snow had fallen again, and the lane itself was covered in white, but the alleys were protected somewhat by the overhanging buildings, most of which were multi-level homes. The sounds of the busy city were sparse here and the area had a distinct loneliness about it. Few people were about in the open; smoke was rising from most of the chimneys nearby.

Victoria pulled her cloak tighter around herself.

"What exactly are we checking for?" asked Malak, looking about the lanes with disinterest.

"The alley where they supposedly knocked out a thirty-stone man," said Victoria.

She stopped, casting her eye over the reports again. She turned first to the Corpse Warden's report, reading over the case notes; they were similar to what had been noted by the Militia-Sanctioned Mage and the Death Wardens.

Massive wound to the lower jaw, into the mouth and brain. Kill-wound. Signs of heavy impact to front of skull.

"Enough to knock him out," Victoria murmured to herself. She turned toward her colleague. "Malak, question. What weapon would you use to knock a man unconscious?"

Malak shrugged. "Club probably, easy enough. Proper strike right round the back of the head, and down he'd go."

"I agree," Victoria replied. "A simple club would do it, but the wound would be smaller, no more than a bruise. Not large, and the girls made no mention of a weapon. How did they do it?"

Malak smirked. "Could have tried putting his fat head through a wall; that'd do the job."

Victoria nodded. "Possibility."

Malak didn't hide his confusion. "I was joking," he said. "No way a youngster would have been able to manhandle a bloke that large."

"Maybe she didn't manhandle him at all." She tapped her forehead. "Maybe she got him to charge her and he brained himself?"

Malak appraised the alleyway. "He'd need a run-up though, surely?" He indicated by looking up and down the lane. "Lane's not wide enough for a proper run, and neither are the alleys. It would take a while for a lad that big to gain speed."

"True," Victoria admitted. "Not enough room here. Whatever they did, it would have had to have been at close quarters." She cast around again. "Malak, start checking the alleys."

"For what?"

"Signs of struggle, like I said."

Malak shook his head but moved to comply. "And as I've already asked, you really think we'll find anything this long afterwards?"

"Worth a try, surely?"

With Malak moving to the right, Victoria moved to check the alleys to the left.

ALYSSA

The first alley was a definite no go. It was stacked with wooden crates and they seemed to have been there for a while, their surfaces worn and damp. The second alley was no better, with wine barrels and long planks of wood haphazardly placed around it. Frozen cobwebs indicated none of the stuff had been disturbed in a long time.

The third alley was muddy much as the rest but relatively clear of anything that would get in the way. There were plenty of footprints in the mud and doors off to the left and right. She checked the walls. Several wooden crates were stacked up by the entrance of the alleyway, just inside it. At just around head height one of the crates' sides had caved in, the timber broken inwards, as if something heavy had impacted it; something a roughly circular shape.

"Malak, over here," she called.

He trotted over and blinked when he spied the impact point. "Interesting," he mused.

"Put your head in it," she ordered.

"What?"

She nodded at the cracked crate's side. "Your head's around the same width as the drunk's skull. See if you fit."

Still confused, Malak moved in front of her and steadied himself with his hands on the wall. He set his forehead carefully into the broken timbers. He fitted convincingly.

"We have our knock-out blow."

"But how the hell did they manage that?" Malak said, straightening up. "She would have needed the strength of ten men."

"Two girls not enough?" Victoria asked, with a rare smile.

"Hardly," he snorted. "I've taken guys down before. You need a hell of a force. Besides, that would be easy to stop."

"How'd you figure?"

He held up his hands, then, head down, he leaned his palms on the wall again. "As long as I put my hands out to stop you, you can't bash me."

"But if we immobilize his hands…" Victoria mused. She checked the report but there was no mention of the drunk's arms or hands. No wounds or bruising visible. "How would you have done it?" she asked, as she looked up.

Malak shrugged again. "Grab his arm, put it up his back, then wallop. Down he'd go."

She slipped the reports into the inside pocket of her cloak and presented her arms. "Show me."

He gave her a sideways glance.

"Show me, *carefully*."

He took hold of one of her arms and motioned for her to turn around. Slowly, with deliberate care, he pulled her arm up, so that it was held at an uncomfortable angle up her spine. She grimaced.

"You all right?" he asked; his breathing on the back of her neck was laboured.

"I'm fine," she assured him. "Can't move the arm, so that works. Now what?"

"I'd just use my other hand and shove you forward."

"Okay."

He paused. "Ah…you sure?"

"Hell's depths, man, I thought you were a soldier? Besides," she teased, "thought you'd like having a woman at your mercy?"

He took the back of her head in the palm of his hand and pushed her forward. She flinched, her eyes involuntarily shutting. When no impact registered, she opened them to find Malak had stopped just as she was about to hit the wall beside the crates.

"Like that." There was a certain professional satisfaction in his voice. "Real quick, giving them no time to stop themselves with the one hand. Best they could do would be to cushion the blow with their free hand, but that would probably just break a few fingers."

He let go. She loosened her arm in its socket, letting the feeling return.

"So, she'd need a lot of muscle to both immobilize him *and* smack him into something. Our problem is we just don't know how an eighteen-year-old girl managed to do that to a guy three times her weight and size."

Malak peered at the wrecked crate again. "I've no idea," he admitted. "If she were any other race, maybe dwarf, even some elves or fey."

He found Victoria staring off into the middle distance. "Aye," Victoria wondered presently. "What other race…" She trailed off.

"I know where you're going with this, Victoria." Malak crossed his arms. "But to me…and I'm repeating myself here, *she* just doesn't look like a vampire."

"And again, Malak," Victoria countered, "I don't believe they *have* a standard appearance."

Malak cleared his throat before he spoke again. "Are you really going to go to Horna Gladwell and start the conversion with 'So, there's this barmaid.'"

"First, that's not how I sound." She wagged a finger. "And second…" She stopped for a moment, then let out a long breath. "You…just might be right."

Malak blinked. "What was in that meat you ate?"

"Don't get used to it," Victoria warned him. She inspected her notes again. "We need more evidence." He glanced up. "Right, come on, you."

"Where to now?"

"The Archives," she confirmed, heading for where they had stopped their coach.

Malak groaned. "Victoria, me crossbow…"

His colleague's pace did not falter, and Malak was forced to run to catch up with her.

CHAPTER 7

THINGS AS THEY ARE

"Vampires, vampires," muttered the wiry librarian as he led Victoria and Malak through the maze of tall bookshelves. Rolls of parchment, leather-bound books, piles of papers; everywhere was covered in history.

"How do they keep this all organized?" whispered Malak to Victoria.

"Courier fey mostly," answered the librarian ahead of them, though he continued to cast his squinted eyes over the latest shelves the small group had come across. "They flutter from shelf to shelf, organizing, cataloguing." He chuckled. "It's a game to them. The accumulation of knowledge. They enjoy it."

He returned to his search. "Now…" He adjusted the large pair of multi-lenses glasses mounted on his wrinkled face before scrutinizing the note he had with him. "Should be around…eh… here!" Aged hands reached for an especially thick tome, bound in red leather. He passed the book across to Malak. "And this one." He gave Malak another book, smaller than the first but in similar burgundy leather. "And this one." He passed a total of eight reference manuals to Malak.

"That will start you off, I think." The librarian's smile was open beneath his balding scalp and wrinkled brow. His long arms motioned them back the way they had come. "Reading tables are to the rear of the building, not too far. Please keep the noise down; we're still a library, after all." He coughed, pushing his glasses back up the length of his nose. "Our official closing time is later this afternoon, but, as you have the necessary clearance, you are free to stay as long as you wish."

"Thank you," Victoria said. "Come on, Malak."

As they walked away from the librarian, Victoria asked, "You all right with those?" indicating the stack of books Malak was carrying.

"Of course," he assured her. "They're just books. Heavy, well-built, big books…"

Victoria smirked and Malak slowed his pace. "All right, sod it, take a couple off the top."

"Lightweight," Victoria chided but helped her colleague anyway.

Later, they were seated opposite each other, the books the librarian had acquired for them arrayed around them, plus additional notes and material Victoria had found. Both of them shuffled on the stiff wooden stools they were seated on.

"These things are bloody terrifying," Malak whispered.

Victoria nodded her agreement. "Listen to this," she said, reading from the book she had open in front of her. "*Ragnor the Ravenous earned his name during the Terror wars, waged 100 years before the Six Nations War. Those who fought against him report that he was impervious to harm, blades, arrows and bolts bouncing off his skin as if it was made of stone. In one battle, he single-handedly killed over 100 men and horses. The source of his impervious nature was never found."*

"That's a proper nasty piece of work," Malak commented.

"You're right enough there." Victoria shook her head and leaned back. "No wonder they considered themselves Gods."

"I've not read a single positive thing about any of them, not one." Malak cast his hand over the papers before them.

"The evidence is overwhelming," Victoria agreed.

"What's their play, though? The drunk guy, why take his blood and then kill him?"

"Presumably to cover up the fact that they'd taken the blood in the first place."

"It's still a bit out in the open, though?" Malak made a face. "Hanging him up on the spikes? Why murder him publicly? They could have just killed him and chucked him in the river."

"I've been thinking the same. It's too...showy." She whirled a hand. "Like they want us to know."

"Why?"

The question lingered even hours later, as Victoria put the finishing touches to a 'vampire reference' she had built up. She dropped her quill into the inkpot. Malak was just returning to their reading table. He had two tankards of clear water with him, one of which he set down in front of his colleague. Victoria nodded a thank-you.

"Okay, so I've got together what I can see as 'common' vampire traits: here goes." By the flickering light of the oil lanterns on their table, Victoria began her explanation. "They need fresh blood to survive, which they acquire by drinking it through their fangs, which can grow to a huge size."

"Lovely," commented Malak.

"They're unnaturally strong and fast, as well as being practically immortal. If they continue to get the blood they need, they can live forever."

"So far so nasty."

"Here's the kicker." She looked over at Malak. "They can be anyone. Once turned, vampires don't age. They just remain the same, except when feeding…" She shuffled through some of the older papers on the desk until she found one and held it up for Malak to see. "…when they look like this."

Malak recoiled from the artist's impression, drawn on the parchment. "Wouldn't be hard to miss that in a line-up."

"Yeah." Victoria turned the paper, regarding the print herself with a similar grimace. It showed a man with his mouth agape. He would have been a normal-looking human, if not for the fact that his canine teeth were extended out past his chin into pin-prick points, and his upper jaw grossly distended ahead of him.

"What else is there?" She returned to reviewing her findings. "Unnatural strength, enhanced resistance to external damage, some magical immunity, incredible speed and some kind of… best way I can describe it is a kind of aura of dread?"

"Dread?"

"According to this, when close to normal humans, they cause a feeling, one of the stories describes it as 'a creeping dread running up your spine, a sensation of foreboding, the chill or fear of the grave.'"

Malak held up his tankard, his face tense in thought. "Are we applying all these traits to the girl Alyssa?"

Victoria sighed. "Yeah," she answered, after a pause.

"The teenager we met at that tavern," Malak said. "The same tavern that tried to kill us with food?"

Victoria sat back again, grabbing her tankard as she spoke. "It's a bit too convenient, isn't it?"

Malak took a sip before nodding in the candlelight.

"She doesn't appear to fit the stereotype we're building up," Victoria said.

The two investigators sat in silence for a while. The candles flickered, casting shadows over the shelves of books arrayed around them. The early winter night had settled in now; the windows nearby were black and shuttered.

"Let's get your crossbow," Victoria suggested at length, finishing her tankard. "Maybe the trip out will give our brains a rest from all this research."

"It's a bad thing when I'm so distracted by work I forget about Bess."

"I'm sure she's fine, Malak," Victoria reassured her colleague, with a slight twinkle in her eye.

"I just don't like leaving her on her own so long," Malak bemoaned. "Out in a stranger's house, surrounded by stranger people…"

"All right, all right, we're going. I don't need another whinging match." Victoria gathered her things. "Ye know how to lay it on thick."

"Got you moving, didn't it?"

"Grab the books, you ass, we'll drop them back."

ALYSSA

✝ ✝ ✝

"Ah, Katy." Gretna approached the young girl. "There you are. Glad to see you again."

"Hello," Katy greeted her new boss. Katy had just slipped shyly into the kitchen from the outside, her eyes darting about. Five other barmaids were in the extensive kitchen, all busy doing their jobs.

"You all right?" asked Gretna, frowning up at the girl.

"Fine," Katy said, immediately. "Ah, it's just…"

"Out with it, girl," ordered Gretna, hands moving to hips. "I don't have time; we've a busy night ahead. Militia are holding a retirement party for one of their number, so the place is going to be packed."

Katy paled visibly. "Oh," she managed. "Great. Alyssa's outside," Katy went on, "in a corset."

Gretna's frown changed from impatience to confusion. "And?"

"She'd rather you inspected it…before anyone else does."

Gretna's frown remained but she nonetheless marched to the door, closely followed by Katy.

Outside, she found Alyssa, her eyes darting about as Katy's had before, with her grey cloak pulled tightly around her. "You can stop doing that," ordered the dwarf, her impatience increasing. "What's the matter?"

"I got a corset. It's just…it's…"

"For the love of all the Blessed Dwarf Gods," muttered Gretna, "just show me!"

Alyssa apprehensively opened her cloak and revealed what was underneath.

It took a long few seconds for Gretna to reply, after simply staring at what Alyssa was wearing. It took a lot to surprise a dwarf, especially Gretna, but she was indeed surprised by the barely-legal spectacle before her. She looked from Alyssa's red cheeks to Katy's wide eyes and then back to Alyssa.

Gretna sighed. "Grograg's name, when I said corset," she began, massaging her forehead with her thumb and index finger, "I did not mean one of those…things! Please tell me you brought a change of clothes," she asked next, casting Alyssa a uniquely dwarven exasperated look.

Alyssa quelled before the dwarf's eyes, shaking her head slowly.

"Told you." Katy had her head in her hand.

"Can I go home and change, please?" Alyssa asked, taking Gretna's reaction as an excuse to wrap up again.

"'Course not," snapped the dwarf. "You're on the clock and I can't spare you. There's a militia retirement party tonight; a lot of hungry men are going to be about the place!"

"Wouldn't that be even more of a reason for her to change?" Katy interjected. "After all, that corset…kind of puts a lot on display."

Alyssa shuddered and pulled her cloak tighter around her.

"We'll keep you in the kitchens," Gretna decided after a moment's thought, tapping her chin. "Make sure none of them see you. In fact, make damn sure they don't see you." Gretna considered things. "They'll think I'm running a brothel otherwise!"

ALYSSA

"Thanks." Alyssa's hands went to her hips as she cocked her head at Gretna. "That makes me feel so much better."

Reluctantly, they went inside, Alyssa keeping her cloak wrapped around her.

"Right, you lot," bellowed Gretna at the girls in the kitchen. All work immediately ceased at her call, all eyes turning in her direction. "Alyssa will be working in here for the night. For reasons that will shortly…" She cast a look back at Alyssa who was already starting to go red again. "…become apparent."

Gretna nudged Alyssa. With much reluctance, Alyssa took off her cloak and hung it on the hook.

There was at first a deathly silence, followed by collective gasps, stares and more than a few open mouths. Sarah promptly fainted.

"All right, quit it, the lot of you!" growled Gretna. "Get back to work." She started barking orders. "Katy, you'll fill in for Alyssa on the tables."

Katy nodded and rushed to the tavern proper.

"Alyssa, you'll take over at the vegetables from Sarah."

"Okay," Alyssa readily agreed as she side-stepped over the unconscious body of Sarah to the worktop.

"Carean, wake Sarah up and make sure she does the floor." Gretna shook her head. "Hayley, make a note in the ledger. 'When staff are asked to wear corsets, they shall be of the traditional undergarment style.'" She glanced across at Alyssa and felt her eyebrows raising again. "Lest we encourage the wrong type of customer," she concluded.

✝ ✝ ✝

"Awfully packed tonight."

Victoria nodded at Malak's comment.

They stood across from the Elk's Horn; the tavern was busy as ever. Around the front, a small crowd had formed. Humans mostly, with a few elves, dwarves and even a few concerned-looking bearkin; the large creatures were motioning to the doorway and shaking their heads. They all, to varying degrees, were wearing either tabards or cloaks in blue and red. They were also all armed and armoured: leather jerkins, with swords and clubs attached at their belts.

Victoria motioned to group with her hand. "Remember the watch house? Larrick City militia," she explained, "probably some lucky sod's retirement. We'll go around the back and get your crossbow through the kitchen," she suggested, "much as I'd like to join them."

Malak's expression of expectation turned to apprehension. "The kitchen?"

"Yes, the kitchen, Malak." There was a pause. "Where the food comes from," she added.

He rolled his eyes. "I know that, woman. Just. The kitchen? The tavern's kitchen?"

"What's the problem?" Victoria demanded, one hand moving to her hip.

"It's just," he rubbed the back of his neck, suddenly nervous. "It wouldn't be right me entering."

Victoria raised her eyebrow. "What do you mean? We'll go in, ask for the crossbow, job done. Heck, they'll probably just hand it to us through the door." Ignoring Malak's looks of disquiet, she led him round the back, trying to find the kitchen entrance. She soon found it, a sturdy oak door set into the side of the tavern wall with a '*staff only*' sign hammered onto it above head height. There was a vision slit just below the sign.

Malak followed, but slowly, his footsteps heavy.

"What's wrong with you?" Victoria demanded.

"It's a Tornar thing," he sheepishly admitted. "Men don't enter tavern kitchens, it's disrespectful."

She blatantly rolled her eyes. "Fine, I'll get it for you." She knocked on the door. "But you owe me."

Presently the vision slit slid across, revealing a pair of ice-blue eyes. The background noise of a busy kitchen was immediately apparent. The eyes blinked with confusion.

"Sorry," said a female elfin voice, hesitantly, presumably belonging to the eyes, "the bar entrance is round the front."

"Council of Peace," said Victoria, having unhooked her belt clasp and now holding it up for the eyes to see. "We were here last night, and my colleague left his crossbow behind. We're here to collect it."

The eyes blinked again, now looking unsure. "I don't know about that; I wasn't on last night. I could check with the boss. If you'd both like to wait inside?"

"Just me." Victoria stepped forward as the door opened. "I'm afraid my colleague has an unnatural fear of kitchens."

Victoria stepped through the door into a very large kitchen. It was busy; all around her, meals were being prepared by young girls of various species and a single large, out-of-place orc. The same one who had served Malak and her *the* meal. Victoria suppressed a shudder.

"I'll just find the boss," said the tall, blond elf maiden who had opened the door, before she darted off through one of the kitchen's doors into the tavern itself. Victoria stood near the door as the girls around her moved to and fro, busy with their work and hardly noticing her.

Quite suddenly, Victoria felt an oddness, a sudden feeling of apprehension creeping up her spine. She frowned.

She twisted to find one of her suspects, Alyssa, just about to bump into her.

Fortunately, the collision never happened, as Victoria rather deftly grabbed the plate the girl was carrying, preventing it both from hitting her and its carriage of chopped tomatoes from spilling all over themselves.

"Woah," she stopped the startled girl. "Careful."

"Oh, I'm so sorry…" Alyssa began. The girl's eyes went wide. "Oh," she said, in a surprised and weak-sounding voice. "Hello."

Victoria's eyes dropped to what Alyssa was wearing. "Ah!" she exclaimed. "It's…nice to meet you miss…ah…"

"Alyssa," Alyssa confirmed, going red.

"Yes, Alyssa."

The two of them stood, Victoria looking over Alyssa's shoulder, Alyssa's face blending in with the tomatoes she was carrying and both of them still holding the tray. Around them, the other serving girls seemed not to have noticed.

"Um," said Alyssa presently, after a few seconds, "sorry, but I need to pass these on."

"Oh yeah, of course," responded Victoria, her momentary shock abating, as she let go of the tray. "Sorry," she apologised and managed to get an eyeful again.

"Sorry," Alyssa echoed. "Slight clothing…problem," she stammered, before hastily moving away.

ALYSSA

Victoria breathed a sigh of relief. She felt the unpleasant feeling leave her, turning to see the girl hurrying into another part of the kitchen.

"Here's your crossbow," came a voice. Victoria glanced down to find the female dwarf from the previous night holding up Malak's K-12.

"Ah yes," said Victoria. "Sorry about that."

"No bother." The dwarf had one hand on her hip. "It's lucky none of the customers nicked it. Anything else?"

Victoria glanced around to where Alyssa was now collecting fresh vegetables.

"Uh, hello?"

Victoria blinked, realising she had been staring off at Alyssa.

"Sorry. Many thanks." She shouldered the crossbow.

"No problem; anything for you folks!" The dwarf led her out. "Make sure to tell your colleagues if they want good food, they come here!"

"Of course," Victoria lied.

The door gave a rattle as it closed behind Victoria. She looked back at the door, eyes taking on a faraway look. Then she handed the crossbow to Malak as he approached, without turning toward him.

"Uh-oh," he said after checking the weapon over, noticing Victoria's distraction. "You're doing that thinking thing again, aren't you?"

She glanced at him and nodded. "Walk with me."

Malak fell in beside her as they headed back to the coach.

"Met that Alyssa girl," she began.

"Oh, up close?"

"She nearly bumped into me."

"Lucky she didn't," said Malak.

"I felt…something." Victoria glanced left and right as she and Malak crossed the lane to the waiting coach. "Uneasy. Chill up my spine."

Malak nodded with understanding. "You think it was her?" He took her hand as she offered it to him, helping her up into the coach.

"Exactly," she said, pulling him up before leaning back into the coach. "Remember what we read in the Archives?"

"Aura of dread?" Malak suggested.

"That's the one. Right now, we can attribute two unnatural characteristics to that girl. Unnatural strength and an unusual aura."

Both Victoria and Malak made the same face.

"Still not a lot to go on," he said.

Victoria nodded her reluctant agreement. "Still no real evidence."

"Not been in this game long but last time I checked, even Council of Peace needed some kind of proper 'ard evidence."

"Yes." She regarded the tavern again. "When do taverns close?" she asked.

"About two, I reckon; that's the latest. Why?"

Victoria frowned, crossing her arms. "I think it would be useful if we found out where this girl lives. I'm thinking maybe following her home might be an idea."

Malak shrugged. "I've nothing better to do. Got one request, though."

"Name it."

He smiled. "Let's go eat first. At a different tavern," he added hastily.

CHAPTER 8

THEN THINGS CHANGED...

James arrived later that evening. Gretna took some persuading but eventually let Alyssa go and meet her boyfriend.

She slipped out of the kitchen and soon found James in a corner by one of the smaller tables. He smiled warmly up at her as she sat, though his expression turned to confusion when he noticed she still had her cloak on in the crowded tavern.

"I have a slight…wardrobe malfunction," she said, flicking her hair back nervously.

"Okay." He smiled again.

"How are you?" she asked.

They talked. Despite being in a busy tavern, they were not disturbed by anything around them.

He talked about work mostly. To Alyssa it was interesting, hearing about how the steam engines of the docklands worked and how *great advances* were being made for the betterment of everyone. It seemed that James was responsible for both forging and installing the cogs he worked on, then testing the various machines with steam or by hand. It was all so magical-sounding, to her ears at least.

He let her talk as well, keen to know more about her, but she told him only so much. Some of it true, some of it not. Her life as an orphan, her time in the Sarakin orphanage, her time as a barmaid.

It was he who had to go in the end, his face gloomy when he glanced at the wall mounted time-keeper set above the bar top.

"Will you be back later?" she asked, eyes hopeful through her glasses.

He shook his head solemnly. "We're working into the late hours tonight. Big transport project," he explained. "They're converting the Argon Legion Airships for civilian use. Removing the cannons, installing new…" He stopped himself. "I'm boring you."

Alyssa vigorously shook her head. "I'm a barmaid," she explained, with a slight smile. "As I've told you before, what you do is *not* boring."

He breathed easy. "Well, anyways, because it's late hours I won't be back. I'm sorry."

Alyssa felt her cheeks going red for a reason other than the garment under her cloak. "I'm glad we met up again."

He leaned in and kissed her, only quickly.

"Thank you," Alyssa said, a little taken aback. Her smile grew.

He turned to leave but she put her hand on his arm. "Wait," she said. "Ah…I have an idea. If you like?"

He nodded. "What are you thinking?"

"Would you like to walk me to work tomorrow?"

"Yes," he agreed, almost immediately, smiling again.

She beamed at him, reminding him of her address again and agreeing on a time. Then she leaned forward and pecked him on the cheek.

A silly grin spread across his face as she left.

Alyssa headed back toward the kitchen, passing Katy and getting a grin and thumbs-up; Alyssa returned the grin. She opened the door to the kitchen, closing it behind her and slipping off her cloak. As she hung it on the rack, she turned just in time to bump into Sarah.

"Sorry!" the other girl said immediately before looking down and promptly fainting.

Alyssa rolled her eyes. "Oh come on, really?" She frowned down at the now-unconscious girl. "Again? It can't be that bad." She found the rest of the kitchen staring at her. "It is that bad, isn't it?"

The kitchen, as a whole, nodded.

She sighed despairingly, finding her hand fidgeting with her glasses again. Alyssa hugged her chest and slid over to the vegetable preparation area, resolving not to leave it for the rest of the night.

☩ ☩ ☩

The embarrassment and tension of the night began to dissipate as Katy and Alyssa made their way home.

"I'll escort you," Alyssa had suggested, and Katy agreed once the tavern had closed.

The two girls trudged through the snow. The streets were quiet now; the girls found themselves alone as they dodged snow drifts and pools of frozen water.

"Glad we can talk now," Katy said as they made their way through the night.

"So," Alyssa began. She lowered her voice. "Ghost seer?"

Katy shyly nodded. "Yeah. Runs in my family."

"You can all…?"

"We can all see dead people." She chuckled. "Funerals can sometimes be strange affairs."

Alyssa shook her head. "I just…you don't seem like a seer."

Katy smiled up at Alyssa. "You don't seem like a vampire."

"Thank you. How does it work?" Alyssa asked, after a minute.

"It's as if you're looking through a window all the time," the young girl explained, eyes squinting for effect, "with something smudged against it. Most days I just see normal people, but sometimes I see figures. They're out of focus but there. I have to concentrate to see them."

"Ghosts?"

Katy bobbed her head. "Amongst other things, but mostly ghosts. And ones like you."

Alyssa caught herself. "Other vampires?"

Katy made a face. "Actually, no. You're the first vampire I've encountered. What I mean is people with something different about them."

Alyssa pursed her lips. "So, I really am…dead?"

Katy nodded solemnly. "At least technically, I think," she added.

"It's just." Alyssa rubbed her forehead. "I sweat, I blush, I don't seem to smell, of, like, a corpse."

"I don't think we'd be getting on as well if you smelled like a corpse," Katy assured her.

Alyssa smiled. "Thanks."

Katy studied her new friend. "Does it hurt?" she asked.

Alyssa frowned.

Katy pointed to the side of Alyssa's mouth. "The teeth. I can just see them," she pointed to either side of Alyssa's nose, "up into your head. It must be that you morph when they come out."

Alyssa turned away. "You…don't want to see that, Katy."

"I wasn't suggesting…" Her hand was on Alyssa's shoulder. "Sorry, you don't need me being that curious."

Alyssa swallowed, pursing her lips. "I don't like it."

"I know," Katy said.

"When they come out…" She closed her eyes and stopped for a moment. Katy halted beside her, her hand still on her friend's shoulder. "This will sound stupid, but," Alyssa took a breath, "every time James and I…kiss." She paused. "He's in danger," she said in a low voice.

For a time, the two girls did not move or say anything. Alyssa stared into space, her features pale even in the dark. Katy watched her, brow furrowed in concern. The moon looked down on them and the clouds maintained their slow slide across the starry blackness.

Eventually both breathed and resumed their walk, silent for long moments.

"My dad works at the city library," Katy informed Alyssa suddenly. "I say this because we might be able to do something."

"What about?"

"About you being a vampire."

Alyssa smiled again. She sighed. "That's appreciated, Katy, but I've done something like that before. I've researched, I've been through a lot of books. There's not a cure for being a vampire."

"Don't be so sure," Katy said carefully. "There's a place in the library. A secret place, a vault. They keep the forbidden stuff down there. It might be worth a try."

Alyssa shrugged. "Why not?"

They found themselves at the end of Katy's street.

"Thanks for walking me home, and the chat," Katy said.

"Thank you." She returned Katy's smile, though it was subdued. "See you tomorrow night?"

"Yeah, I'm on," the other girl confirmed.

They shared a hug. Katy seemed to want to speak more, but reluctantly she turned to go to her house.

Alyssa watched her go. She wiped her eyes, sucking on her lower lip. *You're in danger too,* she thought. "A little hope is a dangerous thing," she mused to herself before turning away. "Glad you didn't give me too much of it."

✝ ✝ ✝

"At last," muttered Smithy, watching the girls split off.

He had followed them from outside the tavern, not daring to enter with so many militia men about. He had assumed the girl would be on shift again and he had been right. Now, at last, she was alone.

His hand found the hilt of his blade inside his ragged coat. He smiled with ugly teeth. "Hold her up, get the coin," he said to himself eagerly. "I'll corner her at Wardens Alley."

He hurried off.

✝ ✝ ✝

Her cloak wrapped around her, Alyssa hurried through the night, keen to remove the offending corset in the comfort of her home, keen to forget most of the night.

At least Vlad had been quiet the last few days.

A scruffy-looking man stepped out from a side alley, stopping Alyssa with a start. In his hand he was brandishing a rusty knife.

"Right, girly," he slurred from behind a cloth that he'd pulled over his face and waving the blade clumsily. "Hand over the coin."

Oh for God's sake.

Alyssa eyed the man, looking deep into his eyes. "You look familiar," she said, unconcerned.

He pulled the cloth a little further up, over his nose, grunting. She stepped forward.

The mugger flinched back, as if forgetting that he was the one who was armed and dangerous. "Don't get all ballsy with me," he growled, recovering himself. "I'll gut you. Hand over your coin."

"You were at the tavern," Alyssa said. "You were sitting with the other docklands workers a couple of nights back." Alyssa rather pointedly crossed her arms and glared at him. "I should have known you'd be trouble, you had that look about you."

This defiance seemed to utterly confuse him for a few seconds. Then his eyes glared. He let the cloth drop from his face, which was now contorted in rage, his lips pulled up in a snarl.

"That's a shame for you," he said clearly now. "Can't have you telling the militia that."

He swung for her.

Almost casually, her arm shot out and grabbed the blade, sharp side on. Smithy had the briefest moment to blink in surprise before Alyssa strengthened her grip and snapped the blade in two like a pencil. "Idiot," she muttered and smacked him across the head, hard, with the open palm of her other hand, the blow knocking him out cold before he hit the ground.

She sighed. "They never learn."

She checked the hand she had grabbed the blade with. Nothing, not even the smallest mark. She bent down and pulled him up by his shirt, looking him over.

The Craving...

It has been a few days.

The already dark street seemed to darken further. Shadows shimmered and moved around Alyssa. In the alleyway from which the mugger had stepped, two red lights blinked into existence, and coils of blackness spilled onto the pavement.

Drink him, came Vlad's familiar voice, an echo on the wind.

"Perfect timing. Hello, Vlad," muttered Alyssa, rolling her eyes.

Drink him, insisted Vlad more sternly. *This is no time for foolish morals, girl. I commend your restraint in the tavern but if you want to survive, you must feed. Who better than this creature? What better state? What better time?*

She eyed the unconscious mugger, the man effectively hanging limp from her outstretched hand. Then she cast her eyes about. She couldn't see anyone at either end of the long street, and her sharp hearing could detect nothing except the ambient sounds of a city asleep.

His neck was exposed, his head hanging to one side.

Her mouth opened. Her needle-pointed fangs extended at her mental command, flashes of long white bone jutting forth from her upper jaw with a hiss. Her jaw elongated to an unnatural size, her lips pulled back and her teeth morphed.

Blood is life, Vlad advised her. *Take his blood. Take it all.*

She leaned forward, and the teeth penetrated the man's neck. She drank.

She shuddered as blood was willed into her, a cascade past her tongue. She blinked away tears, her body shivering as the life-giving liquid filled her.

Take it all, Vlad willed her, joining in the sensations inside her. All around her became as nothing, fading into blackness, fading into blur and tendrils of dark motion. There was only she and her victim. She would take him for everything, she decided.

Give in. Vlad's voice was strong; stronger than she remembered him ever being.

I... she tried to speak in her mind.

...am...the...

Her own words seemed muffled, as if speaking underwater.

...master...

Give in!

Her eyes bulged in their sockets, rolling over red.

Suddenly some blood gurgled up, bubbling from her mouth. She stopped, her mouth agape, the teeth still in the man's neck.

James.

A single word spoken through her mind.

131

ALYSSA

What would he think if he saw me?

The eyes rolled back to their natural colours. Fresh tears rolled with them, cascading down her cheeks in a sudden stream.

She pulled her teeth from the man.

Gods...no...

The mugger's body was limp, his skin deathly pale. A sudden fear gripped her, and she tossed the mugger one-handed across the road, letting him roll into a pile of rubbish, snow and discarded fruit and vegetables sitting to one side of the road.

Her teeth were pulled back into her and her face returned to normal.

Except for the splatter of blood upon her lips and chin. A single pale hand went to her mouth; it came away red. "What have I done?" she breathed.

You have become what you were always meant to be, came Vlad's voice in unwelcome confirmation.

She stepped back, nearly tripping over her own feet. "No... No, please no."

Vlad's shadow rolled back into the alleyway. It seemed to be smiling.

I will leave you to think. Contemplate. Accept, he said. *Summon me when you are ready to take the next step, my acolyte.*

He was gone; the streets were as they should be.

Alyssa was alone.

Panic set in.

She looked to her bloody hand, shiny and wet with red. Hurriedly she wiped it on her dress. Her head snapped left and right, seeking any who could have seen her. She saw no one.

Fear in her heart, she ran.

✝ ✝ ✝

Victoria and Malak stepped out from the alleyways on either side of Jackal Street. They exchanged looks as they crossed to the middle of the cobbled street. Both of them had their mouths slightly open in shock.

"You did see what I just saw, didn't you?" asked Malak, cradling his crossbow, his voice carrying an edge of fear. His head snapped in the direction he had watched Alyssa go.

Victoria nodded slowly, gripping her pistol, staring off in the same direction.

"She pierced that guy, then tossed him across the road like a rag doll," Malak breathed, now looking to where the mugger's body lay motionless.

"So casually," added Victoria.

"Don't know about you," Malak said, pointing his weapon at the man, "but I don't feel like being put in that guy's position."

"Agreed." Victoria regarded the slumped form of the would-be mugger. "Though we better check him."

"Moving," confirmed Malak, bunching his shoulders and keeping his crossbow aimed in the direction that Alyssa had gone as he crept toward the body. Victoria kept low as she dashed straight across the street to the pile of rubbish.

"He's still breathing," Victoria reported as Malak moved to her shoulder and stood guard. She was crouched by the injured man. "I'm no healer, but I'd say he's lost a lot of blood. Look."

Malak looked down to where Victoria was pointing at the man's neck. Two small lines of crimson marked where Alyssa had bitten him.

"He'll be feeling that in the morning," she said.

"You think he'll live?" Malak asked.

"Maybe. Better summon the militia. Them and a good apothecary."

"He'll need a bath or ten," Malak remarked. "What's the plan?"

It took Victoria a few moments to reply. "Malak," she said carefully, "I don't think it's wise to keep following her to her house." She glanced over at him. "Or maybe lair's a better term."

Malak nodded.

"We don't know what else she's capable of," Victoria continued. "We'll stick with knowing where she works and go from there."

Malak breathed a sigh of relief. "As much as I've gone toe to toe with everything from orcs to bearkin," he said, giving her a look, "I prefer to know more about what I'm fighting."

"Agreed."

"What do we do next?"

Victoria's frown deepened. "Once everything's sorted here, we give the Overseer what he wants. The definitive answer."

☩ ☩ ☩

Above Victoria and Malak, two figures watched from the rooftops.

The two investigators departed, walking quickly back the way they came.

One of the rooftop figures nodded from beneath his hood, the motion barely visible in the night. "Excellent," he said, and looked to the one beside him. "Remember, she is to be taken…"

He paused for a moment; there was the faintest hint of a smile in the way he spoke the next words. "…as undamaged as possible. She must be conscious for what comes next."

"It will be done, noble Leader," confirmed the other figure.

"So I will it," the Leader spoke, "so shall it be."

☧ ☧ ☧

Victoria watched as Horna stroked his chin.

She and Malak stood in the Overseer's chambers in front of his extensive desk, having just arrived and handed over the report to their commander.

Horna's eyes scanned over the pages as he flicked through them one by one, a pair of small spectacles balanced on his nose. The two candle holders behind him were lit in the darkness, as well as a lantern on his desk, affording him the necessary extra light to read at the late hour. He was making a point of ignoring his two employees.

Malak stood with his hands clasped behind him in his military 'at ease' whilst Victoria stood more casually, arms by her sides.

Presently, Horna set the papers down and took his glasses off. He rubbed his eyes before looking at both of them. "A definitive answer," he agreed after a few moments. "You have confirmed that there is indeed a vampire on the loose in the capital."

"Yes," said Victoria, her expression neutral.

"Very well." He set the report on the desk. "My men will take it from here."

Victoria frowned, exchanging a puzzled expression with Malak.

"Isn't that us?" Malak ventured.

Horna smiled; it was a knowing, evil smile.

"No, my dear Malak," Horna said. "I mean *my* men."

☩ ☩ ☩

Victoria sat, using her knife to poke the food around her plate in front of her. The sign on the wall of the Broken Dreams tavern had read "Freshly cooked good food."

Victoria frowned and sat back from the plate.

It was the next morning. They had been dismissed by Horna immediately after filing their report and he had set to work making his plans. Victoria had not slept well. "His men," she muttered to herself, frowning down at her food.

She felt eyes on her and looked up to find one of the barmaids, a petite, young auburn-haired girl, staring at her.

"Everything ok?" the girl asked timidly.

Victoria shrugged. The girl approached and leaned toward her in a conspiratorial manner. "The sandwiches are a safer bet." Her voice was a hushed whisper, casting the plate of what appeared to be corned beef in front of Victoria an embarrassed nod. "I make them. If you want?"

"Why not," sighed Victoria, allowing the girl to collect the plate.

"Back in a sec," the girl said.

Victoria watched her go. "Short, young, beautiful, and potentially hiding any number of secrets," she mused. "Wonder if you're another vampire." She shook her head with a rueful smile and didn't notice Malak approaching.

"There you are." He took a seat in front of her and set his crossbow to one side.

"Aye, here I am," she replied, "and please don't forget that thing again." She nodded toward the crossbow.

"Thought it odd when I was early to work and you weren't," Malak remarked. "I take it you don't like where things are going?"

She nodded, sighing, her face wearing an expression of both resignation and disgust. "All he's going to succeed in doing," she said, "is either getting a lot of people killed or, at the very least, giving the Council of Peace an image of conflict instead of peace." She leaned back in her chair again, crossing her arms and staring at the tavern ceiling. "A raid." She addressed the ceiling. "A bloody Darnhun raid." She looked at him again. "Subtle," she concluded without conviction.

"I know," agreed Malak. "They always leave a mess."

"What is it they say?" Victoria asked, folding her arms. "The Darnhun are the only ones who fought *everyone*?"

"Aye," Malak agreed. "They'd that naval fleet and those damned moving castles."

"My brother fought them," Victoria said. "He hated them. Every one of them could fight. From the lowest healers to the highest commanders."

They sat for a moment. Malak flashed a grin. "Now, a Tornar raid…"

Victoria smiled at that, easing a little.

"They'd do it right," he continued, smile growing. "In and out quick, proper slick. Dead or alive, we'd have it done, no worries. And best of all…" He began crossing his arms smugly. "…no civilian casualties. Now that, that is professionalism."

Victoria nodded. "If only. Pity it's only Kane Maldor that uses your lads."

They were quiet for another moment.

"If even half the stories from the archives are right," Victoria said presently, "there *will* be civilian casualties tonight."

Malak nodded. "I still can't believe it, though, even after all we've seen. That girl. A vampire? She just didn't seem the type, you know?"

Victoria shrugged. "They're known to be deceptive creatures. She could be a few years old or centuries old. We wouldn't know either way."

"Suppose," lamented Malak. "You really think it's going to be a disaster?"

Victoria nodded solemnly.

"What's our plan then?"

Victoria looked over at him. "We do our job. Make what preparations we can. As distasteful as it is, we make sure the Darnhun at least have our reference notes. Maybe one of them has enough of a brain to take precautions."

At that moment the sandwiches arrived, the young girl setting down a wooden plate of brown bread, packed with what appeared to be fresh corned beef, lettuce and a sweet-smelling sauce.

"Thank you," said Victoria.

The girl curtsied. "And for the gentlemen?" she asked, smiling over at Malak.

Victoria answered for both of them. "Two James Black Water. Straight."

The girl blinked.

"I know it's early," Victoria told her. "But we'll need the liquid courage."

CHAPTER 9

ENTER THE DARNHUN

"Thank you for walking me to work."

James and Alyssa were at the kitchen entrance to the Elk's Horn. It didn't take long to walk to the Elk's Horn from Alyssa's house, but they made it last.

It was only now, with James about to leave her, that the memory of what she had done the night before once again rose to the fore.

"Working late again?" she asked, distracting herself.

"Yes," he said, a distinct sadness in his voice. "But I was thinking, maybe I should take some time off. Meet with you during the day sometime?"

She'd known that was coming. "I'll see what I can do. We'll sort something," she reassured him, flashing that smile that she had found melted him each and every time. She was not disappointed.

"Yeah," he said, grinning, then seeming to recover. "Yeah," he repeated, clearly trying to pretend he hadn't just completely fallen for her.

ALYSSA

She swallowed, her lips tensing.

"When you two are quite finished?"

The couple turned in unison to find Katy with her hands on her hips, her head tilted to one side and a cheeky smile on her face. "Some of us have work to do tonight."

Alyssa and James moved to one side of the door. "I'd best go in and get started," Alyssa said to him. She leaned in, giving him a peck on the lips. Then another, just to be sure, and another for good luck; they were more earnest, yet careful, than previous times. She forced herself not to continue.

Katy was shaking her head at them, the pink ribbons in her hair flickering in the moonlight.

"Bye," Alyssa reluctantly bid him farewell. "See you tomorrow."

"Yes," James said, still dazed from the barrage of kisses. The two girls left him swaying slightly as they entered the tavern together.

"He is new to this, isn't he?" said Katy as she and Alyssa hung up their cloaks.

"Oh yeah," agreed Alyssa, checking her apron, relieved that tonight she wasn't wearing a corset. "But I'm teaching him," she added.

Katy again shook her head. "Remind me which of us is older again?"

Just as Alyssa was about to move off, Katy caught her by the arm and pulled her close. The ghost seer looked into the vampire's eyes; the vampire blinked. "You okay?" the young girl asked.

Alyssa's expression dropped. She glanced about before lowering her voice. "I thought I was hiding it."

"What's wrong?"

"I can't…I can't keep existing this way." She inhaled, looking to the door. "I'm getting great at acting like everything's fine." She looked back at Katy before quickly wiping a tear that had pooled in her eye. Her voice broke a little as she spoke again. "But…I did something last night after we…and…it's just hard."

Katy pursed her lips. "What I told you about…" She glanced past Alyssa; Gretna was entering the kitchen. "We'll talk later," she assured her friend. "I promise."

She scurried off to the assignments board mounted on the wall listing the girls' various tasks that night.

Alyssa took just a moment to compose herself. She checked her hair, glasses and eyes. She wiped a few more tears that threatened to fall and took a deep breath. *Right, ready.*

Impressive.

Vlad's sudden voice sent a shiver down Alyssa's spine. No darkening of her surroundings had heralded his voice; she could not see his evil eyes anywhere.

Your powers of seduction have improved. James would make an excellent thrall.

Alyssa swallowed. "Thank you," she managed in a faint whisper.

I will disturb you no longer. I only seek to…compliment the improvements I have seen.

The pressure inside her skull left her. She breathed, catching herself again.

I will start work, and I will do my best.

☩ ☩ ☩

ALYSSA

Victoria peered around the corner. Down the street lay the Elk's Horn; business was, as usual, in full flow. Its lights were bright, the tavern packed with customers.

"Lots of people," muttered Malak.

They were awaiting the arrival of the Darnhun mercenaries and Horna. Their coach was parked nearby, out of sight. The night wasn't all that cold, the expected snow not yet falling. Victoria had dispensed with her usual cloak and was just in her tunic and leggings. Her pistol and sword lay on her belt, and Malak had his weapons with him, his K-12 locked and loaded on a sling over his shoulder.

There was a low rumble in the distance: the noise made by heavily laden horse-drawn carriages.

"Here they come," warned Malak, taking a step into the relative safety of the nearby wall.

Victoria did the same. "They like to make an entrance."

Two huge horses rounded the corner of the street entrance, snorting fog-like smoke, both in full plate armour, the metal jet black in the moonlit night and lined in dirty silver. Behind them, four more horses appeared in the same polished metal. They pulled a huge war carriage, black as the horses and of a spiked, evil appearance. It was a vast rectangular thing, disturbingly like a coffin in shape. Metal blades and hooks lined its flanks, upon which were mounted weapons: swords, axes, and long-crossbows. Where the light of the moon caught it, jagged runes of bronze glinted from the few points not covered by its deadly cargo.

An identical horse-drawn carriage pulled up behind the first. Upon the flanks of the carriages, a stylised symbol was stenciled.

Coiled sapphire snakes, two of them, twisting round each other, heads pointing outwards.

"Viper Kin," Victoria spat with malice, "not just any Darnhun then. Cut-throat mercenaries."

The thundering hooves came to a halt near where Victoria and Malak stood. Just as both carriages halted, the Darnhun emerged from the rear doors. They were tall, heavily armoured warriors, clad in scale mail and thick rounded shoulder pads of boiled leather. Their armour was darkened like the carriages that bore them. Their belts and chest harnesses were festooned with small wooden cubes with fuses hanging from them.

"That's a lot of Thunderboxes," Malak said in a hushed whisper.

Over their bodies, crossbow bolts were slung from strips of leather, and daggers sheathed at ankles and shoulders. Each man had a short sword secured in a sheath hanging from one hip and a flintlock pistol on the other. The pistols were compact things, none of the elegance of the weapon Victoria carried; they were meant for the press of close quarters with multiple barrels of a dull silver colour.

Their helms, though, were by far the most distinctive feature of the formidable-looking fighters. Short-nosed and pointed, with two small red eye lenses that glowed inwardly and mouth grills that gave a menacing air to an already frightening appearance, they were almost insectoid.

Each man brandished as his main weapon a Bolt Spitter: black, ugly repeater crossbows. They were short, no longer than a man's outstretched arm, with fat boxes of bolts slung underneath them and short daggers attached to the fore grips. They were angular things, all sharp lines, just like the men who carried them.

Amongst the Darnhun was Horna Gladwell himself. He was clad in layers of thick white fur over his council robes, making him appear larger than his normal short stature. He seemed at ease amongst the warriors around him, shaking a few by the hand as if meeting old friends. He peered over at Victoria and Malak in surprise, but his expression quickly changed.

"Ha," he said, nodding curtly as he approached the two of them. "There you are. Anything to report?"

"Nothing." Victoria deliberately shifted her gaze from Horna to the Darnhun troops behind him. "What's your plan?"

"Simple," he said. "We will enter the tavern and arrest her."

"A lot of people about," Victoria pointed out. "Might make things difficult."

"I doubt it," he replied with a touch of malice. "Anyone stupid enough to get in their way…" he nodded back at the assembled Darnhun. "…will regret it."

"What of our reputation, sir?"

"Have no fear," he assured them. "They may not look it, but they can be discreet. Now," he added in a distinct tone of arrogant authority, "you two are no longer required. You are dismissed for the night."

Victoria and Malak exchanged perplexed expressions.

"No backup?" Malak asked.

"We won't need it," he said. "I have more than enough men."

"Sir," put in Victoria. "We don't know what this girl is fully capable of."

"Yes, we do. It was in your report. That handy reference you created, what was it, common vampire traits?"

"We've only observed her for barely a few minutes," Victoria countered, her frown deepening. "Only the Gods know what else she can do. These things have unique abilities, so the scriptures say…"

He raised his hand. "It matters not. By the end of tonight, she will be in custody and this will all be concluded. As I have already ordered," he continued before she could speak again, "you may go."

"With respect, sir," Victoria said. "I think we'll stick around and see this through."

Horna frowned, but only briefly. "Very well. You may observe. Silently, I might add. Do not get involved. Understood?"

Malak and Victoria nodded. Horna turned on his heel, walking back to his soldiers. Victoria stalked back to the coach and swung herself up into the carriage passengers compartment, slamming the door shut. Malak kept a respectable distance, entering on the opposite side from his colleague.

"Harcan!" Victoria barked once they were both aboard. "Park this crate round the back so I can see the kitchen door."

"You think she'll do a runner?" asked Malak as he sat opposite her.

"That," she said, "or we'll get to watch a few of those idiots fly through the wall."

✝ ✝ ✝

ALYSSA

This has been okay, thought Alyssa. She felt a little more at ease now; Vlad had kept his word and had made no further comments.

The tavern business was good, with just the right number of customers not to overwhelm the bar staff. Her mood had lifted now that she was out on the floor, where she had the most fun and Katy was alongside her, learning some of the ropes. The previous night's events had receded into the background.

I'll wait until night's out to speak with Katy about it, Alyssa thought.

"That's Christopher," Alyssa said now, nodding over to a young man seated in the corner. "Single, he's training to be an actor. One of our regulars."

Katy raised an accusing eyebrow. "Are you trying to set me up?"

Alyssa's eyes betrayed her. "No…no, just, introducing regulars."

"Who happen to be single?"

Alyssa fumbled her words. "Ah, well."

"It's okay," Katy assured her. "It's appreciated." Katy looked around for a moment before leaning in, as if to whisper something to her friend, but then Gretna appeared.

"Enough mouthing, you two," grunted Gretna. "Double order for table three. Medium steak with extra greens. Someone got a raise down the docklands."

Katy and Alyssa took the trays handed to them.

They turned toward the tables in unison just in time to see the front door explode.

The door disintegrated with a thunderous boom and blinding flash of ruby red light. Sawdust and chipped wood cascaded outwards over those nearby. Tables, chairs and people were bowled over, thrown to the floor. A couple of the other barmaids close to the door when it exploded were blown clean off their feet, one slamming into a wall, the other catapulted onto a table. The air was suddenly thick with debris.

Thick smoke billowed outwards, engulfing everything in its path, coiling around the support beams as people coughed and spluttered in the aftermath.

Katy and Alyssa stood in shock, mouths agape.

Time re-asserted itself.

Black shapes thundered into the tavern through the blasted door frame.

"Everyone on the floor now!" bellowed the first tall, heavily armoured man to enter, in a thunderous demanding voice chipped with a foreign accent. He wore jagged leather armour and brandished a wicked-looking crossbow, the lenses in his pointed helmet glinting a demonic red in the candlelight.

Everyone with any sense did exactly as told; those not already on the floor were diving for it or crawling away from the new visitors, spilling drinks. A total of six warriors entered, all dressed identically to the first and carrying the same ugly weapons. No one challenged them, all in the tavern too shocked or injured.

Darnhun. Vlad's voice came anew in her head; he sounded almost impressed. For once the pain of his existence in her mind did not bother her. *Be careful,* he warned.

Katy, Alyssa, and Gretna were the only ones who remained standing. Alyssa and Katy still had their huge trays of food and Gretna stood defiant.

"On whose bloody authority?" bellowed the dwarf, marching across the tavern toward the unwelcome arrivals. Six crossbows swung to point at her. Gretna stopped slowly at the centre of the tavern, raising her hands.

"My authority." It was a muted voice, but it indeed had an edge of authority.

The two Darnhun nearest Gretna parted to allow the owner of the voice to enter from the direction of the obliterated entrance. He was a well-dressed man in furs, with a bald head and grey moustache. He picked his way carefully over the blasted remains of the tables and chairs, as well as the occasional injured person.

He smiled that superior, arrogant smile that men of power possessed and regarded Gretna thoughtfully. "I do apologise," he said. "But we are here for one of your bar staff. We have come for Alyssa."

"Why?" Gretna demanded. Alyssa didn't need to see Gretna's face to know she'd be red with rage.

"She's a vampire," the figure stated bluntly, casting his eyes around.

That aroused a few low mutterings from the clientele; Alyssa swallowed nervously. *Oh no*, she thought.

For once we are in agreement, concurred Vlad.

"We are here to arrest her," the man said. "Where is she?"

Alyssa's eyes shifted to Katy. Katy was casting her a sideways look; her features had paled, and she licked her lips nervously.

Vlad, seeing we're on pleasant terms for a change, any ideas?

It was slightly sickening to Alyssa to be conversing with Vlad, but the situation gave her little choice.

This location is too crowded, he cautioned. *Your powers would be observed by too many. For now, escape is your best option. Run.*

"Where is she?" the man repeated, impatience evident in his tone.

Behind her, Alyssa heard the kitchen door open. She chanced a look and spotted three more of the Darnhun entering, crossbows aimed. Beyond them, the back door to the outside. It was closed but near to hand.

Alyssa's eyes, full of fear, looked back to Katy.

"Run," Katy mouthed.

Alyssa hesitated, even as she heard the Darnhun behind her moving further into the tavern. She could move fast when she needed to, inhumanly so, with sudden bursts of incredible speed; faster than the eye could blink.

She let go of the plate and turned, twisting into a low crouch as the tray started to fall. Pushing off from the floor, she rocketed through the open inner door, into the kitchen, a blur of motion.

Three more Darnhun were in the kitchen, watching over the remaining terrified barmaids. With one of them in the way, the door to the outside closed behind him. She barrelled into him as she landed, her speed and strength belying her lithe body as she knocked him to one side into one of his comrades, both landing in a heap near one of the worktops.

She spun round in her low position and swiped at the door through which she had just entered, knocking it closed. She was rewarded with a dull thud, the door closing on one of the Darnhun as he tried to come in after her, knocking him back. She turned to face the third Darnhun, who had enough time to drop his crossbow on its sling and draw a wickedly barbed dagger. He brought it round to swipe at Alyssa. She ducked under the slash as she balled a fist and awkwardly punched upwards, into his chest. It was enough, though; she heard him cough as the wind was knocked from him and he fell away.

There was no time to lose as she crouched down in front of the door to the outside.

I hope this works.

☩   ☩   ☩

"That was quite an entrance. How long do you think it'll take them?" asked Malak, idly casting the tavern another eye.

"Oh, I'd say…" Victoria began, but was interrupted as the back door of the tavern burst apart. Splintered wood exploded outwards, carpeting the street behind the building in a cloud of fine sawdust. A single figure was silhouetted for a moment, crouching in the fog of the explosion.

Victoria and Malak stared.

The figure stood in the half light of the tavern windows.

"…now," Victoria finished, as she and Malak exchanged a quick glance.

"Alyssa," breathed Malak.

Alyssa started running, darting off toward the nearby alleys. Victoria and Malak leapt from the coach and chased after her.

As she ran past the door, Victoria glanced inside. Three of the Darnhun troopers were down on the floor. Others seemed to have just entered the kitchen and were scattering out of the tavern.

Victoria dashed onwards as the Darnhun fanned out and

Horna roared angrily into the night. She and Malak rounded a corner as Alyssa ran on, blindingly fast.

"Malak, engage!" Victoria ordered, drawing her pistol. Alyssa's speed made her only a moonlit silhouette in the distance. She heard the distinctive click of Malak flicking the safety catch off his crossbow. She moved to the side to give him a clear shot as they raced after Alyssa through the streets, quickly leaving the Darnhun behind.

Behind her Malak stopped, dropping into a crouch with practiced speed. He took a breath and pulled the trigger on his crossbow. There was a thud as the drawstring sprung forward, unleashing a bolt. It rocketed forth, emitting a dull scream as it streaked past Victoria. Up ahead there was the sound of a bolt hitting flesh, a wet splat.

Alyssa kept running. So did Victoria.

Malak sprung back into a run. He quickly caught up with his colleague.

"Take her down!" Victoria ordered.

As they turned down another street, Malak skidded into a crouch again onto the muddy ground. There were two more thuds as he unleashed more bolts in quick succession. Their harsh squeals echoed in the night as they were launched toward their prey.

Again, Victoria heard the sound of the projectiles impacting, but still the girl kept going. Alyssa was at the end of the street and turning left. Victoria and Malak ploughed on, reaching the end of the street themselves and sliding around the corner, weapons up.

Ahead of them, in the gloom, a running figure disappeared into another side street.

ALYSSA

"Double back," Victoria ordered. "We'll catch her in a crossfire."

She ran on before Malak could argue. His footsteps receded in the other direction and she increased her pace, heading for the side street. She slowed as she rounded the corner with her weapon up and out, but stared into an empty street.

† † †

Alyssa had been aware of something hitting her but had kept running regardless. She knew she could outpace any human in a sprint, but this wasn't a sprint, and her pursuers seemed to know this. *This is a cat-and-mouse chase; I'm the mouse.*

She'd ducked into a side street and was looking round for a hiding place amongst the wooden crates that were stacked along the walls.

They'll expect that, Vlad advised.

Fine time for you to chip in!

They are still after you, the spectre advised. *They will search this ground level. The roof, now girl!*

Without arguing, she crouched down, then sprung upwards, impossibly high, almost as if her body weighed nothing at all, defying gravity. She landed lightly into a couch, then knelt upon the roof and waited, listening.

Alyssa hazarded a glance over the lip of the flat roof she had landed on, looking down the street. She spied them. The two hunters; the same two she'd seen in the Elk's Horn a few nights past. Victoria and...the guy. She'd not caught his name. They were moving away. She hoped they'd not seen her.

Victoria had her pistol pointed out in front of her, moving cautiously into the street Alyssa had just vacated. The woman pointed, motioning to her colleague, who moved to check a nearby alleyway with his crossbow. She then moved to check the crates along the wall.

Thank the Gods, thought Alyssa.

You are a God, Vlad advised her, a certain humour in his voice.

Alyssa ducked down and crept on all fours, slowly, to the far end, away from where she'd seen the two of them going. She could make good her escape now. Still moving with as little noise as possible, she kept low and crawled over to the lip of the flat part of the roof. She then leaned over and put her feet down onto the slanted, slate-covered sides of the building. All she need do now was jump down and she'd be away.

Carefully, she slowly began to stand. She spread her legs with care, cautiously rising so as not to over-balance herself. She stood to her full height, then bent her knees, ready to make her jump.

Her only warning was the crack as one of the slates directly underneath her shoe broke in two.

She squealed as she felt her footing slide out from under her. The roof gave way at an almost leisurely pace, at least as far as it seemed from Alyssa's point of view. But there was nothing she could do to stop her fall. She fell on her backside and slid down the roof after the slate, making a thunderous racket.

Damnation! hissed Vlad as they dropped.

Alyssa landed in a heap amongst the shattered roofing, but as fast as she could she jumped back up onto her feet.

"Malak, on me!" Alyssa heard the woman yell behind her from further into the alleyway.

ALYSSA

Alyssa ran as fast as she could, doing her best not to slip on the broken remnants of the roof. She darted into a side street as soon as she could, but was aware that the woman was following her. She rounded into another connecting lane and dashed into it.

Wheelbarrow. Down, now!

Alyssa did as Vlad told her, crouching behind a large over-turned wheelbarrow to her left.

She waited.

She heard the footsteps.

No more delays, no more excuses. This is about your survival.

Vlad's eyes materialized in front of her, the black nothing-ness closer than she had ever seen him. His two red eyes were clearer and more menacing up close: two red cuts of blood against the blackness. His misty black existence dominating her view. With difficulty, she stared him down.

When she approaches, strike. I do not sense her colleague; he has not given chase. Her weapons will do you no harm. Take her, drink her, end her. Quickly, before the other one realizes his mistake!

She shifted backwards, and the pressure lessened for her.

You. Have. No. Choice.

He emphasised each of the words, his voice taking on a dark finality.

She glared back at him, tears glinting at the edges of her eyes.

Victoria's footsteps grew near, slow on the cobblestones.

Alyssa prepared herself. She slid one foot to her side, making ready to stand as fast as she could. She spread her arms.

Be quick, came Vlad's last suggestion, before he faded from her vision completely. She felt free to do as she willed.

As Victoria passed the wheelbarrow, Alyssa acted.

One second Victoria's pistol was held beside her, at the ready; the next it was pointed upward toward the sky. Not by Victoria's hand, but Alyssa's. The young girl had moved from her hiding place with incredible speed and grabbed Victoria's gun hand, pushing the weapon away.

Victoria reacted, her other arm going for a clumsy left-handed draw of her rapier. It would have worked, too, if Alyssa had only one arm; however, she had two perfectly functioning arms and stopped Victoria's attempt easily. Victoria tried to struggle, to break free, but Alyssa knew her formidable strength. She held her pursuer in a vice-like grip.

Victoria jerked her right leg up, bringing her knee straight into Alyssa's stomach. Alyssa didn't even blink. Victoria, on the other hand, cringed in pain, gritting her teeth.

Alyssa glanced downwards, but after Victoria's rash action, her head rose slowly. The two women's eyes met. Victoria stared into the young girl's eyes; Alyssa stared straight back.

Victoria was at Alyssa's mercy.

Do it, Vlad's voice came. His spectre hovered just over Victoria's shoulder, watching.

"Just get it over with," Victoria hissed with a last act of defiance, turning her head so that her neck was exposed.

Alyssa's upper jaw once again grew monstrously, like the canines of a bear, as she opened her mouth. The two-pointed fangs slid forth from Alyssa's upper jaw, growing to a spot just an inch from Victoria's throat.

Victoria grimaced before squeezing her eyes shut.

It was as if all of creation stopped and stared.

ALYSSA

Alyssa's eyes were open, looking past the swell of her mouth to the pale skin of Victoria's neck. Precious seconds passed. She did nothing.

Do it! Vlad urged again, his menacing ghostly visage rushing over and dominating Alyssa's view beyond Victoria. The power of darkness coiled around both her and Victoria, though Victoria gave no outward sign that she was aware of it.

You have no time!

But Alyssa did not move. Quite suddenly, she started to cry.

Victoria opened one eye; she blinked.

Tears were rolling down Alyssa's cheeks past her glasses, even as she stood like a statue, mouth still menacingly agape, lips pulled back from her horribly distorted jaws, the two huge pointed teeth extended. It was both tragic and oddly comical.

You failure, snarled Vlad, his presence shifting into the shadows, leaving only hatred in its wake.

Alyssa sniffed and suddenly let go of Victoria, stepping back.

Victoria caught her breath, hand instantly to her neck. Breathing slowly, she stared at the girl.

Alyssa's head was down again, rivers of tears still flowing, pooling around the rims of her glasses. She was sobbing, the massive sharp fangs protruding just past her chin shuddering as she cried.

Victoria holstered her pistol and let go of her sword, the blade sliding back into its scabbard. She reached forward and, with an incredible amount of care, placed her hand on the girl's shoulder. Alyssa seemed as surprised by the motion as Victoria was at making it, tensing slightly at the touch.

"You are a strange one," Victoria mused, her frown deep on her brow.

Alyssa removed her glasses briefly to wipe her eyes, looking up as she did so. "Guou gon't know the half of git," she sniffed.

"You...might want to pull those in?" suggested Victoria tentatively.

"Gorry," said Alyssa, doing so. The fangs slipped back up into her head with an odd slurping sound. Her jaw shrunk down to its normal size, her upper lips rolling back and her whole face shifting back into place.

Victoria shuddered.

"This wasn't supposed to happen," Alyssa started, fresh tears rolling down her now human-sized cheeks. "I had a boyfriend and... and a best friend..." She trailed off, then burst into tears again, sobbing. For all the world she seemed as if she was another frightened and miserable teenage girl. She covered her face with her hands, ignoring Victoria's shock. "I felt human for once!" wailed Alyssa.

"All right, all right," Victoria assured the girl. "Just calm down, will you? Take a seat."

The alley had a variety of crates and barrels scattered haphazardly about, giving them plenty of places to sit. They chose two low crates sitting beside each other. Victoria carefully led the sobbing girl over; she had relaxed a bit, though one hand was resting on her holstered pistol.

They sat. Alyssa felt like a bedraggled teenage girl. She was aware despite her state that her glasses weren't sitting right, and her hair was a mess now, tossed about in her mad dash for escape. Whilst her eyes weren't reddened from crying, the tears had left lines across her pale features and small puddles of water around the glasses. Almost tenderly, Victoria brushed the strands out of the girl's face.

ALYSSA

"All right," Victoria said as Alyssa started to get control of herself. "I'm not great at counselling stuff so bear with me. Tell me your story."

Alyssa removed her glasses, wiping her eyes with her tunic sleeves. "It was a year and a half ago, I think," she began, her voice still broken. "Just before the peace. He took me from my bed in the orphanage." She sniffed, swallowing. "I awoke but he used something to put me to sleep again," Alyssa continued, absent-mindedly rubbing her arms. "When I woke up again, he'd already changed me. I don't know how. I…I felt awful." Her eyes took on a distant look. "He said I could no longer eat or drink normal food, that I'd have to drink blood. Human blood. I was horrified, said I'd never kill anyone. But he said that I didn't need to, I would not kill. Only drink enough to function. The killing, he said, would come later."

She smiled despite her tale. "He seemed so kind." Alyssa looked away to stare off again. "Like he regretted changing me. That I was special. I liked that part at least." Her face darkened as the memories of that dark day returned. "That was before I realised he was a liar."

All was still around them. No sounds of running feet. No sounds of anything. Around them, their only company were the drifts of snow.

"Go on," urged Victoria.

Alyssa shrugged. "A couple of days later, the heroes arrived. I remember because I was in the throne room. They burst in. They were so fast." She swallowed. "It was so…brutal. They killed anyone who got in their way, with magic swords and fireballs. He stepped forward to fight them. I watched them kill him. Watched the others change back. I thought it was all over, thought I was free. Then I must have fainted, I just blacked out. Next thing I know I'm lying in a coffin in a warehouse near the docks." She screwed up her face. "That wasn't fun. I never did find out how I got there, but I got out right and quick. I had a note with me. It just read: 'You're the last.'"

"The last vampire," Victoria confirmed.

Alyssa nodded. "As far as I can tell, anyway. I've not met any others. Some of the things he or his lieutenants taught me before they killed him, I remembered." Her tone had changed, speaking the word *killed* with more venom, shocking herself. "Avoiding sunlight, drinking blood, being mindful of the aura." She turned to Victoria. "You know…the creepy feeling you get around me. You feel it, don't you?" asked Alyssa, her mournful face betraying a certain hope that the answer would be no.

"Yes," Victoria said plainly. "I can't lie, it's there."

Alyssa nodded solemnly, sighing. "Figures. Since then," she continued, "I've just been sort of existing." Timidly she fixed her glasses again. She hugged herself, face cast down.

"Did you kill the fat drunk?" Victoria asked suddenly.

"No!" Alyssa looked up immediately at the question. "I've never killed anyone. Honest!"

"What about when you're…" She pointed to Alyssa's jaw.

"Oh no." Alyssa shook her head vigorously. "I just drink enough to survive, I never drain anyone…"

"So, you've drunk before?" Victoria pressed her.

"I have to." Alyssa spoke in a regretful tone. "To stay alive, or exist, or whatever you want to call it. I drink from, well, bad people." She gave a smile. Victoria looked back with a neutral expression and Alyssa cast her eyes down again as she continued to speak. "Muggers, thieves, even murderers and crime bosses. I normally go for them when they're asleep, or unconscious. I drink enough to keep me going, but not enough to kill. I figured, if they're weak, well, they won't be able to be as nasty."

"A public service?" ventured Victoria.

Alyssa smiled, a proper smile this time as she met Victoria's gaze. "Yes. I try. I'm not that great at it, though."

There was silence for a few moments. "I'm losing it," Alyssa stated in a low voice.

"What?"

Alyssa looked Victoria in the eyes; she held her gaze. "My humanity," she said. "I've tried to stay...decent. Tried to set rules. Tried to live some kind of life. Tried not to be." She let out a breath. "Evil," she finished in a harsh whisper.

"What about the man last night?"

Alyssa didn't look up, wiping her face again. "You saw that?"

"Yeah, we did." At this Alyssa's eyes rose. Victoria kept talking. "That's kind of why we're here now."

"Did he die?"

"I don't think so," Victoria assured him. "Though I think you've probably put him off trying to mug anyone from now on."

"That's something." After a moment, she asked, "What will they do to me?" Her question was blunt and full of resignation.

"I don't know," Victoria managed, as she looked away. "Prison probably."

Alyssa swallowed nervously. "I don't think I'd be any good in prison."

Victoria looked back at her. Alyssa could feel the other woman examining her.

"I suppose," Victoria admitted, "you don't look like the prison type." She smiled slightly. "Heck, we didn't think you *looked* like a vampire."

Alyssa smiled back.

"I can help," came a voice.

Victoria spun on her heel as she stood, her pistol drawn in a flash. Her weapon found itself aimed at Katy, the little girl with the cutesy pigtails.

"I'm sorry!" she apologised hurriedly, taking a step out of her hiding spot by the end of the alleyway, eyes regarding the pistol barrel with deep concern. "I…I didn't mean to listen in!"

"Katy," breathed Alyssa before covering her mouth. "Oh please, Katy!" Her tears started again.

Katy looked from gun to Alyssa and back again. Tense moments passed and then, completely ignoring the gun, Katy rather brazenly rushed over to Alyssa and embraced her tightly.

Victoria and Alyssa exchanged confused expressions. Victoria lowered her pistol as Katy spoke.

"I'm sorry," she began, releasing Alyssa and looking to Victoria. "I followed you from the tavern. I saw you running off after Alyssa. I wanted to stop you."

"That's…impressive," admitted Victoria. "Neither Malak or the Darnhun seem to have managed that."

"You're full of surprises," Alyssa breathed.

"I know you're a good person," Katy said, turning back and taking Alyssa by the shoulders. There was a great conviction in her voice. "I just know it." She looked back to Victoria again. "I know she's telling the truth. She didn't kill anyone, and she doesn't want to remain a vampire."

Victoria holstered her weapon, but her expression was one of resignation. "I know, but…" She spread her arms. "Vampires. Clear and present danger to peace.'" She lifted her head, casting Katy a look that brokered no argument. "I'm duty-bound to bring her in."

"Can't you just look the other way?" she suggested.

Victoria favoured her with a pitying glance. "Youngster. It doesn't work that way with the Council of Peace. We don't ever do that."

"Why not?" Katy took a step forward, balling her fists. Alyssa thought for a moment that the girl was going to swing for the Council of Peace investigator, but instead, she spoke to her. "She's not evil. She's not going to start another war."

"Yes, but," Victoria shook her head, "it's not my call to make, I have my orders."

Alyssa looked on in mute shook.

"It *is* your call," Katy insisted. Her face was still determined, even though flickers of uncertainty now clouded her words. "You can pretend you never found us."

Victoria chuckled. "Pretend?" She was shaking her head. "What would you do if I was to let you go?" she asked, crossing her arms. Her eyes found Katy again. "Where would you go?"

"I would find something that can change Alyssa back."

Victoria and Alyssa both frowned. "What?" they asked in an odd kind of unison.

Katy looked from one to another, stopping on Alyssa. "You want to change back to human, right?" she asked.

"Yes, more than anything!"

"We find something that can change you back."

Alyssa shrugged, arms out. "Katy, I…" she began. "I've tried. There isn't any way." She lowered her head, feeling the tears return. "I'm stuck this way."

Katy approached Alyssa again and put her hand on her shoulder. With her other hand, she gently cupped Alyssa's jaw and brought her head up so that the two of them were eye to eye. Alyssa blinked at the rather authoritative gesture.

"No, you're not," stated Katy. "We will change you back. That place I told you about in the Great Library. I can get us in. It's what I was going to tell you tonight."

Victoria frowned from behind the two girls.

"He says there's lots of books about magic and magical creatures down in the basement. There's bound to be one on vampires. We can find a way."

"Oh, Katy." Alyssa embraced her friend. "Oh Gods, please let you be right."

Katy hugged her back before turning her eyes toward Victoria in triumph.

Victoria rolled her eyes. "Oh, here we go," she muttered.

"Please," Katy begged.

"Don't ask me to do this." Victoria's hands were on her hips.

"We've got a chance," said Katy, taking another step toward Victoria. She'd the puppy dog look on, augmented by the blond pigtails and pink ribbons. Alyssa hoped against hope that it would work.

"I can't," Victoria said.

Alyssa felt her chest tighten. Then she thought of something.

"There might be another way." Victoria looked past Katy as Alyssa stepped forward now. She put a hand on Katy's shoulder, turning the other girl to face her whilst her other hand went to her glasses, making sure they were secure. Alyssa pulled Katy close and whispered in her ear. "Hold on to me. This might get a bit weird."

Katy complied, wrapping her arms around Alyssa.

Victoria brought her pistol up. "What are you…"

She never got to finish.

Alyssa summoned them, feeling her body morph, the power of the blood she had taken so recently coursing through her. Sudden ripples of purple energy swirled round her, crackling in the air; the smell of burning came with them. They spun around Alyssa and Katy, blurring them.

Then, they came into being.

With a sound of bursting fabric, two huge over-sized bat wings suddenly erupted from Alyssa's back, surging forth in a rain of destroyed fabric. They stretched wide, spreading to fill the alleyway, almost too immense to be contained. Grey-black, twice as tall as a man, stretched on six taloned fingers.

Victoria took a step back, eyes wide in shock. "Hell's depths!"

The purple energy waves disappeared. Alyssa cast the investigator an apologetic eye. "Sorry."

The wings rose and fell with a whoosh of air, lifting them high and wide over the girl's back, then flapped again in a powerful blur of motion to an accompanying thunderous boom. Victoria was instantly blown off her feet as Alyssa launched herself into the air, the wings propelling her upwards. Up and away, into the night sky.

Victoria was blown back such a distance that her flight was

only stopped when she hit a snow drift and sank into it. For the briefest of moments, there was a human-shaped hole in the snow before it collapsed in on her. Rather quickly, the alley was once again silent, with only a soft sound of huge wings flapping, slowly disappearing into the night.

✝ ✝ ✝

Groggily, Victoria came to. "Well," she grumbled as she took in her surroundings. "Sod that for a game of soldiers."

She found herself cocooned in snow, the cold holding her in a tight embrace. Her fingers were freezing; she wiggled them to try and get the blood flowing again. She shifted her shoulders, trying to dislodge the snow. At the same time, she tried to lift her legs that were curled up in front of her, but the weight of the snow held her down. She shifted her hips, slowly rocking back and forth to try to move things somehow.

"Who goes there?" yelled a voice, muffled, coming from in front of her, beyond the walls of white around her.

"Malak?" Victoria asked.

"Victoria?"

"Malak! Help me! Get a bloody shovel!"

Victoria heard the sound of snow being shifted.

"Where the hell have you been?" she demanded, shivering.

"I pigging lost you after you yelled," Malak's voice came, clearer now. "Went down the wrong alley, then another wrong alley, then..."

"Fine!" barked Victoria. "Some tracker you turned out to be. I'll wear a bell next time. Just...hurry up."

Soon, Malak's face appeared above her. "Woman," he said, looking down on Victoria's disheveled and embarrassed features. "You must have one heck of a tale to tell."

"Which I will regale you with in full." She tried to shift her body. "After I kick your arse."

CHAPTER 10

HOPE IS KINDLED

A vast shape moved in the darkness of the winter sky. Vaguely bat-shaped in the gloom, it slowly drifted over the rooftops.

Alyssa hoped she was not noticed.

She struggled, her breathing laboured. She was concentrating on both holding Katy with her arms and moving her vast wings up and down in as careful and coordinated a fashion as she could manage.

I hate flying.

She could feel the tattered remains of her tunic hanging limply from her back and was more than a little concerned that her modesty might be in danger if any more clothing strands worked their way free.

It was a nice tunic.

A perfect opportunity wasted, came a voice from within her mind.

Vlad's unwelcome presence returned; the pressure pain from

his anger almost made Alyssa lose her concentration. He was alongside her now, a black cloud keeping pace, red eyes glaring at her.

Give it a rest, Alyssa muttered inwardly, glancing over at the cloud before straining to wave her wings up and down frantically to clear another rooftop.

That woman will not give up. She will pursue you. Your mercy tonight will be your end.

Katy was holding on for dear life. Alyssa's night vision was doing what it was supposed to, and she picked out a landing spot. There was a flat-topped warehouse just below them now, one of the old army blocks now long since abandoned; it would do.

As long as I don't trip.

She flapped her wings and let the air currents pull her upright. She then spread her wings and started to descend.

Perhaps you could at least land properly this time, her unwelcome companion in the sky commented. Vlad seemed either unaware or uncaring at how distracting his voice was.

Alyssa kept the wings spread out and slowly descended towards the roof. Once more, she concentrated. Misty coils of purple-tinged power curled around her. Slowly at first, then quickly, the wings shrunk and were folded and coiled into her, as if her body was morphing them back inside itself. Her body returned to its natural shape.

"Oops." She cringed before she fell rather abruptly the last few metres with a crash.

Katy was still clinging desperately to Alyssa. Only as she impacted feet-first did Katy blink. She looked up from holding on to Alyssa's chest, effectively curled round the girl, to find Alyssa's expression one of intense discomfort.

"Are you okay?" she asked.

"No," replied Alyssa through clenched teeth; her feet were several inches *below* the roof of the warehouse they were on.

Katy let go of Alyssa and stepped back onto the roof, now noticing her friend's predicament.

"Damn," muttered Alyssa. "I liked those shoes."

Katy backed away, giving her friend room. Grunting, Alyssa heaved her feet out of the roof, clambering out of the holes she had made. Her shoes were indeed gone, her feet now bare.

Not my best landing.

Now free of the roof, Alyssa found Katy sitting by the edge of the roof. Alyssa moved to join her and the two girls sat side by side for a few moments. Katy was staring off into the night sky.

"Are *you* okay?" Alyssa asked presently.

Katy turned toward her; her eyes seemed distant, distracted. Her face was downcast. "I will be," she assured Alyssa, smiling weakly. "Just as soon as we get down from here."

Alyssa frowned, then took a look over her shoulder down at the street below. "Whoa!" She practically leapt up from her perch on the ledge. "I didn't know we were this high!" She gave Katy an apologetic look. "Sorry. Again."

I'm apologising a lot these days.

"It's okay," said Katy. "I'm not that afraid of heights."

Neither am I. Not that much.

"But you might want to cover up," Katy added.

Alyssa frowned before looking down at herself and immediately noticing that those last strands of clothing were pretty much gone. She gasped and hugged her almost-bare chest. She looked around for something to cover up with, but there wasn't anything to hand on the roof of the abandoned army warehouse. With a resigned sigh, she remained seated beside her friend.

As long as no-one sees me up here.

"So." Alyssa used one hand to fix her glasses again as the other carefully maintained what little dignity she had left. She dared not meet Katy's eyes. "I'm...ah..."

"Able to fly," Katy completed the sentence. "The wings thing kind of confirmed that." Katy shook her head. "You would think I would have noticed those, but I guess I was too fixated on your teeth." She pointed to Alyssa's back where the ends of the three crossbow bolts still protruded. "Do those hurt?" she asked lamely.

"Not really, no." Alyssa sighed again. "Yeah." She fidgeted with her glasses. "Sorry I didn't tell you about the wings."

"I imagine it's not something you admit to that often. Alongside...being a vampire."

"You and Victoria were technically my first," Alyssa agreed. "Were you telling the truth back there?" she asked next.

As if on cue, Vlad's shape shimmered into existence behind Katy.

Alyssa stared past her friend just before the girl opened her mouth. Katy stopped and stared.

A lot has gone wrong tonight, but I'm going to fix one point right now.

Alyssa screwed up her face. Katy frowned, watching as Alyssa almost seemed to tremble outwardly.

Foolish gi...

Hatred gave Alyssa power, and she channeled it right at Vlad. His red eyes seemed to widen as she concentrated her thoughts into banishing him from her vision.

He shrunk, swifter than ever before; she let her anger give her renewed power.

"What are you doing?" Katy asked, leaning back.

Alyssa didn't answer immediately. She simply shook.

The padlocked chest came into being and Vlad was bundled inside rapidly. He did not resist, nor even speak; he let her conceal and imprison him.

Yeah, you know I'm angry.

Yes, his voice admitted, small and subdued. *As you will, Alyssa the Last.*

Vlad was silenced. "Done," she said with an outward breath, before noticing Katy's surprised expression. "Best that I not explain, think you've had enough weird stuff tonight."

"I suppose." Katy smiled. "What I said *is* true," she said, the conviction in her voice infectious. "Just need to get you into the library at night. It's a bit late now, though, so…." she frowned. "…we need a place for you to stay."

Alyssa thought for a moment. *Can't go to my house. The Council of Peace would probably already be raiding it.* She tried not to think what a mess of the place they'd be making. *Can't go to Katy's, they'll surely record her missing and go to tell her parents.*

"We could try James's house?" Alyssa ventured.

Katy nodded. "Best bet, I guess."

Alyssa stood, rolling her shoulders. Katy passed her an apologetic smile. "Ah, think it might be a better idea if we just find a way down. Because…"

"I'm not any good at flying," sighed Alyssa.

"Yes," Katy agreed, "and you need some clothes."

ALYSSA

After digging Victoria out of the snow drift, they had returned to the tavern. She looked thoroughly miserable. She was freezing from her time within the snow, her immaculate features now oddly highlighted by wet, messy hair and a pale, sickly complexion.

They arrived at the Elk's Horn tavern to find that the Council of Peace delegation had gone. Considering that Victoria was shivering and in grave danger of catching hypothermia, they had wisely decided to get her indoors.

Gretna met them at the now door-less main entrance to the tavern. "What do we have here!" she roared as Malak and Victoria arrived sheepishly, still shivering despite her wearing Malak's cloak. "The Council of *war* has returned! Blowing up my door and injuring my staff! Have we come back to scare the living hell out of my maids again, perchance? Or chase away my customers? Perhaps you'd like to do *all of that* and then some!" She was brandishing a hammer, her eyes ablaze and her colour up.

"Would it help," ventured Victoria, wide eyes upon the hammer, "if I said the raid wasn't my idea?"

Gretna's expression remained, much as the bull regards the red rag, her breathing coming in short, sharp bursts.

"...that I argued against it?"

The dwarf still had the appearance of someone about to tear the head off someone else; her eyes were glaring and her knuckles white as she gripped her hammer.

"And that I'm sure the Council would be more than willing to compensate you for tonight's mistake?"

Gretna raised an eyebrow; her breathing slowed. There was a pause and a pregnant silence.

"Should I say, *today's* mistake?"

Gretna turned her head, both eyebrows now rising.

"Or perhaps…the last three days?"

"My friends!" declared Gretna, casting her arms wide, her face suddenly beaming as if regarding a long-lost family member. "Come in, come in!"

"Finance are going to kill me," groaned Victoria as she and Malak entered.

"Sarah, run a bath upstairs," Gretna ordered to the maids around her. "Bofar, get the vegetable soup going. Unless you two want something more…"

"Gods no!" Malak and Victoria said in unison as they took a seat by the door.

"Anyway." Gretna's expression turned serious. "Your money might pay for the loss of customers and, hopefully, reputation. But what about Alyssa? That true what they said? She a vampire?"

Malak and Victoria exchanged looks of resignation. Victoria nodded. "'fraid so."

The dwarf huffed, crossing her arms and leaning up against a nearby support beam. She shook her head. "I don't believe it. I mean, the girl was so nice! She was my best barmaid."

A couple of the maids around them glanced over. Gretna waved a dismissive hand.

"Oh come on, she was!"

"Well, neither did…" Victoria interrupted herself with a loud violent sneeze that made Malak and even Gretna jump. "Oh gods," Victoria groaned, sniffing and wiping her nose. "Pigging freezing."

"Bath and soup'll sort yeh," Gretna assured them. "What will you lot do now?"

"Hunt her," Victoria bemoaned, her voice groggy. "Official threat to peace, doesn't make it right, mind."

Gretna frowned. "What do you mean by that?"

Victoria winced, having said something she had promised herself she wouldn't. Malak rolled his eyes. "Just tell her," said Victoria, "sod it if I could care anymore."

Malak enlightened Gretna about what had happened with Alyssa and Katy, just as Victoria had told him. By the end of the tale, Gretna seemed a little more sympathetic. Her expression gave nothing away, but her body language was less confrontational. During Malak's explanation, she gave Victoria a rather generous portion of vegetable soup.

The other barmaids had left the three of them alone, busying themselves cleaning the place up after the raid, cleaning up the spills and putting the chairs back up again. One girl was busy attempting to remove a crossbow bolt from the wall.

"Poor girl," Gretna concluded. "Where'd you think she'll go?"

"Maybe that girl Katy's place, but I doubt it." Victoria sipped her soup. She pulled the fur cloak that Gretna had handed her closer around her. "She mentioned something about the Great Library, but I couldn't hear all of it."

"Bath'll be ready shortly, lass," Gretna assured her.

"Never seen you like this," Malak said. "Thought you were one of them proper hardy types?"

Victoria screwed up her face. "You're lucky I'm wrecked," she said, "or I'd kick your ass."

He smirked but said no more.

✝ ✝ ✝

With her clothes hung up in the corner, Victoria sat in a bronze tub filled to the brim with hot water and bubbled soap. She was leaning back, her head resting on the far edge of the bath with her eyes closed and a herbal balm on her forehead. It would help to unblock her nose, or so the dwarf had said.

She had her arms crossed over her chest, the warm water lapping around her naked body. A small table sat beside the bath, with a fresh mug of steaming vegetable soup. Malak and everyone else had been tactfully told not to disturb her on pain of death: the violent, painful kind.

She breathed out and opened her eyes, looking up at the ceiling. "What to do?" she murmured. She uncrossed her arms and pulled herself up into a seated position, then hugged her knees, chin resting on them, letting the herbal balm fall into the water in front of her. "What to do?"

At this moment her contemplations were interrupted as the door opened and Gretna marched in with a collection of towels.

"You know, you could have knocked," Victoria said, turning slightly to cover herself.

"I could have," replied Gretna. "But I then remembered it's *my* bath, in *my* room, in *my* tavern. So, I can do whatever I damn well please."

Victoria sighed. "Indeed."

ALYSSA

Gretna rather brazenly tossed a towel at Victoria. She had to catch it mid-air, holding it up before it landed in the water.

"Bloody hell, give us a chance!" Victoria fumed, having to lean out from the bath at an uncomfortable angle. She swung herself out, splashing water, and rather hurriedly wrapped the towel around her. "And you could have closed the door!"

"I could have," said Gretna. "But then I remembered..."

"Enough!"

Victoria secured the towel and accepted another from Gretna, this time not thrown.

"At least you're in better form now," Gretna said with a smirk.

"I do feel better," she admitted, frowning.

Gretna smiled. "Dwarven brand salts." She spoke with a touch of pride. "Sod your Magra potion rubbish. Dwarf stuff fixes yeh proper."

"Didn't know you were of that profession," said Victoria, starting to dry her hair with the other towel.

Gretna shrugged. "Awful lot you don't know about me, missy, and never will."

"Victoria?" Malak's voice came from the corridor outside.

"In here," she said.

"Yeh decent?"

"Aye."

He entered, then quickly exited, shielding his eyes.

"Gods, woman, you said you were decent!"

"I am, you idiot." She frowned at the empty doorway. "It's called a towel."

"Aye, but you're naked underneath."

There was a pause; Gretna and Victoria looked at each other. "Beg pardon?" Victoria hazarded after a moment.

"A man should never see a woman in nowt but a towel," he intoned as if reading from some etiquette manual. "Unless she's his wife. It's not proper."

"You're a strange little man, Malak," Victoria said, continuing to dry her hair. "If you're not coming in, then sod off and I'll speak to you downstairs."

She heard footsteps receding as Malak wandered back to his post.

"He's a bit of an eejit, isn't he?" asked Gretna.

"Oh yeh. He's a royal pain, but good at his job. Hell of a shot, and he's getting better at the detective stuff."

"That's grand."

Victoria finished drying and reached for the mug of vegetable soup.

"So…" said Gretna as Victoria raised the soup to her lips. "…when yeh thinking of marrying him?"

Victoria snorted, making an unladylike sound and swallowing a mouthful of soup in the process. She set the mug down a bit too quickly, spilling some of it and had to stop herself doubling over. "What?!?" she sputtered, steadying herself. Her eyes watered from the hot liquid spilling down her throat and she gasped as it entered her stomach. Victoria tried to compose herself, coughing and taking in gulps of air. "Dear Gods!" she gasped. "What... what gave you the idea we were lovers?"

"You both like each other." Gretna spread her arms as if the statement didn't need justification. "Seen the looks yeh were giving each other down in the pigging bar. Bloody obvious it was!"

Victoria's eyes widened in both shock and confusion. "Obvious? I just told him to sod off, didn't I?"

"Aye," agreed Gretna, nodding. "And then you told me what a good shot he is and how he's getting better."

Victoria made to reply but her mouth didn't produce any words.

"See, you're thinking now, aren't yeh?" said the dwarf in triumph, tapping the side of her head. "Not just a cloak rack is me."

"Yes, we're partners…I mean colleagues! We work together but we're not…" she paused, "…we're not close," she said next, more quietly.

Gretna crossed her arms. "Yes, yeh are."

The dwarf took a step forward, hands moving to hips and eyes scrutinizing again. Victoria flinched.

"You trust him?"

Victoria nodded slowly.

"With your life?"

Victoria met the dwarf's stare. She rolled her eyes and let out a long sigh. "Yes," she said, almost with resignation. "With my life."

"And he with yours?"

"I suppose."

Gretna nodded. "Then lass, take it from me." She pointed an authoritative finger. "Trust is where it starts and where it ends. Fill in the middle part and you've a partner for life. Don't leave it too long." She thumbed toward the door. "Your man might be an arse, but he's loyal and not a bad looker. Plus, he knows what he's doing."

"Maybe," she allowed.

Gretna shook her head. "Ah! Stubborn. Reminds me of... well, me! It has its advantages and disadvantages. But in love..." She shook her head. "...yeh got to treat them proper."

"Thank you," said Victoria.

Gretna, satisfied, turned on her heel and headed out of the room. She paused at the door. "Besides..." she inspected Victoria, appraising her, "...you're a fancy-looking lass. You've a fine arse on yeh, lovely figure and a fair face, for a human anyway. Any man would be proud to have yeh by his side." She headed on out the door; leaving Victoria blushing.

Victoria stared at the door for a moment. "Dwarves," she breathed, shaking her head, breaking her concentration, then moved to get dressed.

✝ ✝ ✝

Katy knocked on the door again. "Maybe he's not in?" she ventured to the cloaked figure beside her.

"He did say he was working late," said Alyssa's voice from inside the cloak's hood. "But it's almost morning now. Surely he's back?"

The two girls had slipped from alleyway to alleyway, moving slowly and cautiously toward where James lived, keeping out of sight of Larrick City militia patrols. Alyssa had managed to break into one of the clothes shops and acquired herself a heavy cloak as well as a new tunic to regain her dignity. She had left the right coin in exchange, as well as taking time to remove the crossbow bolts from her back. Katy had advised that they were something of a dead giveaway.

Alyssa was still barefoot but she did not mind. It was the least of her concerns.

Now they had made their way to James's house and were waiting for him to answer the door, patiently and at the same time worriedly; dawn was getting close.

I don't feel like exploding right now, thought Alyssa.

The door at last swung open.

The figure of James that stood in the doorway looked like he might explode, if only for a minute. He seemed only just awake, as he was dressed in a faded nightshirt with a night cap on. His wide eyes were bloodshot and his face flushed. He was brandishing a saucepan unconvincingly as an improvised weapon. He had obviously been preparing to yell at whoever was at the door, as his mouth was wide open.

He slowly closed his mouth, his rage at being awoken abating quickly. "Morning," he managed, breathless.

"Morning," said Katy. "Sorry for waking you."

"Ah, that's…that's okay." He was blinking rapidly.

"Can we come in?" asked Alyssa.

"Of course." He seemed to recover a little and stepped back, allowing the two girls to enter. His house was as immaculate as always. Alyssa smiled. She was already feeling a lot less tense just being here. Everything was so tidy. Even the fireplace, with the embers of a recent fire still visible, was well maintained. She could tell from Katy's expression that she was impressed too.

"So neat," she breathed.

"Thanks," said James rather proudly. Alyssa beamed at him.

There was a pause. Each of them exchanged glances.

Eventually, it was Katy who broke the ice. "You're probably wondering why we're here?"

"I am, kind of." He flashed Alyssa a smile.

"We've some explaining to do," Alyssa admitted.

James indicated the dining table and they all sat, James and Alyssa opposite each other and Katy in the middle seat. Katy looked from one to the other. Alyssa and James were staring into each other's eyes. She coughed tactfully.

Alyssa sighed, knowing what she had to do. "James," she said, for the first time finding it difficult to meet his eyes. His warm, welcoming...

Focus!

"I," she began, searching for words. Finally, after tense seconds, she decided to just come out with it. "I'm a vampire."

James hardly moved on hearing what for most people would be incredibly surprising news. He sort of just sat, staring. Not in shock or horror or even surprise; just staring. Alyssa frowned.

"James?" she asked tentatively.

He blinked, almost as if coming out of a trance. "Um." He wiped his face. "What?" he settled on.

"I'm a vampire," she repeated.

What part of that are you having difficulty understanding?

"Okay."

Okay? I tell him I'm a supernatural being and he just nods and says okay? Alyssa frowned, glancing over at Katy, but she shrugged.

"I'm glad you're so accepting," said Alyssa.

Katy studied James for a moment. "You don't know what a vampire is, do you, James?" she asked. Not unkindly, just matter-of-factly.

ALYSSA

"Ah." He made to argue the point but thought better of it. "Not as such, no."

"Oh Gods," muttered Alyssa, hanging her head.

"Sorry."

We are so made for each other.

She sighed. "Okay," said Alyssa, raising her head. "A vampire is a supernatural being that must drink human blood in order to stay alive. Vampires were once human, but through a process…" She paused briefly, then shrugged. "A process I don't know, they are changed into vampires. A vampire cannot exist in the sunlight. They tend to explode." She found herself checking over at James's curtains. They were tightly closed. "They are technically dead, and possess unnatural abilities, such as flying or changing into animals. So." She struggled to find other pertinent aspects to explain. "Ah, and I'm one of them. Oh, and I'm the last of my kind," she added.

There was a delicate kind of silence.

James bit his lip, his eyes switching from Katy to Alyssa and back again. "Ah," he began. "So, you think you're a vampire?"

"Not think. Know," Alyssa corrected him.

Katy rolled her eyes. "Just show him your teeth," she suggested.

Apprehensively, Alyssa did so. She leaned back and allowed her huge fangs to emerge from her mouth. The two bony points jutted toward James from her viewpoint, growing well past her chin. Her upper jaw reached out, threatening to keep going toward her boyfriend, hissing forth, muscles expanding and supporting the growing needles of white. Finally, they stopped, Alyssa blinking with difficulty and holding the odd position.

"So that's what they look like," Katy said, staring.

James reacted differently. His eyes widened, he leaned back in his chair, and after a few seconds of staring in mute shock, he fainted and slumped to the floor.

It was Katy's turn to sigh. "Your boyfriend's a wimp, you know that?"

"Ge is got!" Alyssa said. She pulled the fangs in as quickly as she could.

"This should wake him," Katy said as she crossed to the basin in the corner of the room, taking a cup of water from the bucket beneath it.

"Don't drown him, please," Alyssa said.

Katy immediately emptied it over James; he awoke with a start, sputtering. "Told yeh." Katy nodded at Alyssa as she set the now-empty cup beside her. They were both crouched over James. "One cup isn't going to drown him."

James wiped his face before looking from one girl to another, blinking and gasping. "What happened?"

"You fainted when you saw Alyssa's teeth," Katy informed him.

"Teeth?" He frowned, his expression indicating a quick search of his most recent memories. Then he fainted again.

"Oh for the Gods' sake!" Katy's patience had broken. She grabbed the cup she had used before and stumped over to the bucket again. She returned hurriedly and repeated her actions, pouring the cup over James.

He awoke again, but this time Katy showed initiative. "Don't faint!" she commanded, grabbing him by the cuff of his nightshirt and pointing a commanding finger. Alyssa and James were both taken aback. "Sorry," she apologised timidly, getting up. "I just got a bit impatient."

Alyssa eyed James. "Are you going to faint again?" she asked, not unkindly.

He shook his head.

"Good."

They let him get back to his seat and the three of them sat around the table again. Alyssa wasn't sure where to go from here. James was.

"So," he said, seeming to be more awake and more coherent now after having water splashed over him. "Not human then?" he asked, wiping his eyes.

Alyssa nodded solemnly. "Not really, no."

"You're a vampire."

She nodded again.

He considered this for a while. When he spoke again, it was with acceptance. "Okay."

Katy and Alyssa exchanged the same glances they had used only a few minutes before. "That's what you said before." A frown appeared on Katy's face. "Then you fainted. Twice. After the explanation, you're still okay with this?"

James fidgeted, appearing uncomfortable. "Ah." He looked over at Alyssa. She noticed the look he was giving her. It wasn't angry. It wasn't regret. It wasn't even surprise. "You're not going to eat me, are you?"

Alyssa smirked, despite the situation. "I don't eat people. I just drink their blood, and no," she hastily added, "I'm not going to do that either."

His patient face didn't change. He just nodded, as if that

simple sentence had allayed all his fears. "Okay then," he said. "But that doesn't completely answer why you're here at this time of the night."

Together Katy and Alyssa filled him in on everything. The investigation, the raid, how Katy had met up with Alyssa again, and their plans for the immediate future.

"So, you don't like being a vampire then?"

"No!" Alyssa said, rather automatically taking his hand in hers. "I've been a vampire for a year and a half now and I hate it. I…" She felt tears welling in her eyes again. "…I just want a normal life. I want my life back, I want the sunshine, I…" She stopped, wiping her eyes. "I don't want to have a pair of teeth the size of sword blades and use them to drink people's blood."

James leaned forward and embraced her. Katy put her hand on Alyssa's back, comforting. "It's okay," Katy assured her. "We'll find a way." Determination was in the girl's voice again.

✝   ✝   ✝

Around her, the tavern was closing down. Lanterns were being extinguished, windows boarded up. The orc and Malak were shifting a makeshift door into place at the entrance: one of the tavern's overturned tables.

Victoria had a single small candle burning in front of her. She was sipping a fresh batch of lumpy vegetable soup from a cup. She was staring at the candlelight, frowning.

Malak came up and sat down beside her at the bar top. "They have a kind-of front door now," he announced. She nodded. "You still thinking?" he asked.

"Oh yeah."

"About Alyssa or the raid?"

"Both," she admitted. She took a sip from her cup and sighed. "Darnhun," she said. "Who in their right mind sends a squad of Darnhun to arrest someone? Especially a pigging vampire?"

"We both agreed it was a bad idea," Malak replied, shrugging. One of the barmaids set a tankard in front of Malak, as well as giving him a little smile as she passed by.

"It's more than that," Victoria said darkly. "I've been thinking this through a little…too much."

"Oh dear," groaned Malak. He leaned in closer to his colleague. "Where are you going with this?" he asked hesitantly.

"We've always known Horna was a bad egg," Victoria whispered. "But this…this was bad even by his standards. Why was he so desperate to get her?"

"You think he wanted her for something?"

"Or for someone else?"

Malak leaned back, inhaling through his teeth. "What was it you told me? Means, opportunity."

"Motive," Victoria said. "MMO. Means, Motive and Opportunity. Means was the Darnhun, the opportunity was us. Now, what's the motive? Why did he do this?"

Malak shrugged again. "No idea."

Victoria eyed her cup for a moment. She then stood and raised the cup to her lips to knock back the remaining contents. She swallowed loudly, grimacing. "Still warm," she managed, before thumping her chest and coughing.

"Wasn't quite as liquid as you…"

"As I hoped, no." Victoria breathed out. "Right, let's get home. We'll have some investigating to do tomorrow, but for now, I need a rest."

With that, the two investigators slipped away.

CHAPTER 11

TOWARD A CONCLUSION

All sightings, however obscure, are to be followed up on and investigated fully, read the notice.

It was hung from the archway that led into the Council of Peace Investigation Department building. Within that building was a hive of activity that morning, awash with further Darnhun mercenaries as well as investigators. Darnhun assembled in various groups, being briefed by their commanders. Investigators hurried past, securing weapons or carrying piles of parchment. Archives administrators handed out books and rolls of parchment.

Fortunately for Victoria and Malak, Horna was so busy hunting the vampire he didn't notice the two of them slipping out from the gaggle of investigators and Darnhun troopers.

They headed for Horna's sanctum. "So, you go in and talk to Glynis, and I…?" Malak let the question hang deliberately as they marched side by side through the gardens toward the command keep.

"Talk to Garlow," Victoria instructed.

ALYSSA

Entering the main entrance hall, they found Garlow standing guard by Horna Gladwell's office door. "Victoria?" he asked.

"Here for a quick chat with Glynis, won't be a minute," she said, holding up a roll of parchment.

"You timed that well." Garlow grinned. "He's out, fortunately."

"Almost like I planned it that way," said Victoria with a smile.

As she entered, he heard Malak start his conversation. "I hear you were with the Legions…"

✝ ✝ ✝

Victoria startled Glynis from her desk.

"Oh, Victoria," said the elf, as she hurriedly pushed some parchment to one side of her desk. "I didn't expect you."

"I'm sure," Victoria mused shyly. "You all right?"

The elf sighed, running a hand through her hair by her long-pointed ears. "We're very busy, what with this vampire hunt."

"Yes," agreed Victoria, "odd business. The boss is hyped up about it." She wandered closer to Glynis's desk. "Not sure why, though."

Glynis frowned, her jade eyes blinking. "Vampire." She shrugged. "Clear and present danger to peace, you know that."

"True, but he seems…" She looked at Glynis once she was directly in front of the secretary's table, examining the other woman. "…a little too eager."

Glynis's eyes flickered.

"Why is he so eager, Glynis?" Victoria asked, rather pointedly. "Do you know?"

"No," the elf replied immediately, keeping her eyes on the various piles of papers on her desk.

"Garlow is currently regaling Malak with many, many long-winded tales of his time with the Legions," Victoria explained. She shifted and sat on the edge of Glynis's desk. Glynis looked up as Victoria continued. "So, he won't be bothering us for…" She glared down at the elf, her eyes burrowing into the other woman. "As long as is needed."

Glynis again fidgeted with her curls. "Victoria, I…" she began.

"Can be given immunity in the event of prosecution."

Glynis's eyes widened.

"I've always had my concerns about that evil little man," Victoria said. "But the way he's handling this case suggests more than just a smidge of corruption. This suggests full-blown manipulation by an outside force."

Glynis's voice was a whisper when she spoke. "You can't just make accusations like that, Victoria…"

"Yes, I can." Victoria leaned in. "Particularly when the maintenance of peace is at risk. What has he got himself involved in?"

"Please." Glynis dared to look up this time. "I can't…"

"It's me or Kane Maldor," Victoria stated, leaning back. "But I can assure you, ours will be an informal conversation, but Kane's won't be. That and it'll probably see both of us lose our jobs if anything is found."

Glynis's face had gone pale. "I'll tell you everything."

"Grand." Victoria pulled over a chair and sat down. "Start talking and don't stop until I tell you to."

ALYSSA

"Let's go," said Victoria as she strode from the doorway. Malak made his apologies to Garlow and quickly caught up with her as she breezed past, making for a corridor directly opposite Horna's office doorway. "No time to explain," Victoria said. "Just know this. My hunch was right."

"So now you…"

They quickly came up to a heavy oak doorway. Two Tornarian guards stood either side of it. Unlike the other guards that were usually hanging about, these men were dressed not in overly coloured uniforms but in equipment identical to that which Malak wore: leather battle plate. They looked professional and ready for a fight.

"Yes, Miss Haldred?" asked the leftmost guard, standing at attention but shifting his eyes to look at her directly.

"I need to speak with Kane Maldor," she said formally. "And I need to speak to him right now."

The first thing she saw when she awoke later that night was James's face above her, visible by the candlelight on the bedside cabinet. "Morning," he said.

She smiled up at him. "Evening, I hope you mean."

He nodded with a smile.

Alyssa rose, pulling the covers off her. Around her, James's bedroom was a simple affair. The bed she lay in was spartan and the room blank of decoration. She smiled at the simplicity of it all.

Katy was standing near the bed. She held up a large bunch of keys. "We're good to go."

"I'm so sorry for all the trouble," Alyssa said.

Katy waved a hand. "It's okay. I explained everything to Mum and Dad. The militia and the Council of Peace had already been. We're safe, for a while."

Alyssa frowned. "They were just okay with things?"

Katy pursed her lips. "I might have left out the bit about our plans tonight. I just said I was looking after you, not helping you break into one of the most sacred locations in Larrick City."

Both James and Alyssa continued to look at Katy. "I know I'm awful," she admitted, blushing.

"You okay?" Alyssa asked James.

He nodded. "I couldn't wait to get home," he explained. "Katy and I have been making plans. We've thought about what route to take to the library and when."

Alyssa smiled. She hugged James, then beckoned Katy over as well. "Thank you both." She let them go and moved to the rack in the corner, taking down her cloak and passing the other garments to her friends. "Okay. Let's get going then."

✝ ✝ ✝

"This *still* isn't one of your best ideas," said Malak.

"Yes, thank you for reiterating that," Victoria said.

"Are you sure what you told him…"

"Yes," Victoria confirmed. She had spoken with Kane

ALYSSA

Maldor alone; Malak had been kept outside. "It's clear to him, and the evidence gathered so far is damning. *Very* damning."

"And he'll…"

"I pigging hope so," Victoria interrupted. "He's responsible for 'anti-corruption.' What I told him is his bread and butter."

"And what Glynis said, that's enough…"

Victoria blew out loudly, interrupting Malak. "You are really, really not making this any easier."

It was now late evening. She and Malak kept watch over the Great Library from a nearby side street. Victoria had remembered the conversation between Alyssa and Katy before the vampire had made her escape. The Great Library was their destination.

It was a vast towering structure of pale sandstone, ancient compared to most of the city's buildings. Two huge towers flanked its main entrance, reaching into the sky. They were ornate, with fat, rounded tops, with banners showing alliance to the Larrick City Librarians Guild in the form of a dozen odd glyphs. The front door the towers guarded was a huge affair in and of itself, made of solid oak and studded with iron spikes that would not have looked out of place on a castle. It was barred and locked, and practically impregnable to the average eye.

It wasn't the front door they were watching, though. It was the staff door at the back that they were keeping an eye on, a much simpler door with none of the aggressive nature of the front. It was just within sight line of where they watched from.

"You're doing it again."

Victoria blinked. "What?"

He was looking at her. "You keep staring over at me."

"I am, as they say in the trade, understandably nervous," Victoria admitted.

"That makes two of us."

They maintained their vigil.

"You know we've broken the number-one rule of stake-outs," Victoria said presently.

Malak frowned. "What's that?"

Victoria smiled ruefully. "We forgot to bring any snacks."

☩ ☩ ☩

The three of them slipped through the darkened streets, cloaked and nervous.

They had headed out late, later than perhaps they should have, but none of them wanted to run the risk of anyone still being at the Great Library. Now, through the snow-covered streets, they moved with purpose and speed. It didn't take them long. Indeed, the speed took Alyssa off guard. She looked up at the towering structure. "This it?" she whispered to Katy.

The girl nodded. Hugging the far wall, they slipped across the street and down a side alley. Round the side of the vast structure was a single small door down a flight of steps. Katy brought out a key and unlocked the door after they descended. She looked at Alyssa and smiled. "Okay," she said. "Here we go."

☩ ☩ ☩

"Here we go." Victoria nudged her dozing colleague. "Our customers have just arrived."

ALYSSA

"You were right. Staff entrance, not the front door," Malak said, as he checked his crossbow. "But I've said it once, and I'll say it again. This is not a great plan."

Victoria met his eyes and shrugged. "You only live once."

He chuckled. "Just be careful, all right?"

She looked back at him and pursed her lips. For the briefest of moments, they held each other's gaze. Then they both glanced away.

Victoria slapped him on the arm. "Don't worry about me. Just make sure you're quick."

"All right. Good luck." He ducked back down the side street and dashed into the night.

Victoria watched him go, then caught herself. "Bloody dwarf," she muttered, and made for the staff entrance.

✝ ✝ ✝

Alyssa was glad Katy was leading them.

They had first navigated through the vastness of the main library floor. The dark corridors formed by the dozens of shelves and bookcases had been like some kind of maze. Katy, though, had confidently led them on, directing them with hushed whispers and urging care. Alyssa had thought her whispering a little loud for her liking, but it hardly mattered: there was no one else in the building.

Only when they descended a set of stone steps and she'd opened a door had she given permission to light the lantern they had with them. James had then given the lantern to Katy.

"I know this place," Katy explained, expertly casting the lantern light around. "All the different passageways and corridors. Used to play here when I was younger."

Katy had uttered similar words of confidence during their trip. However, seconds later, the girl smacked her head on one of the smaller wooden support beams that seemed to be placed almost at random in this part of the library's basement halls. "Ouch!" she yelled before her hand was over her mouth.

They all froze. *I hope no-one is actually here.*

Fortunately, no guards burst from the doors on either side of the corridor. After a heart-stopping few seconds, they continued. After somewhat more careful guidance by Katy through the gloomy corridors, they at last came to an ornate iron door, with a keyhole set at its centre and various angular symbols worked into the door's body. Alyssa frowned at the odd entrance way, but Katy seemed unsurprised as she fumbled with the keys.

"Okay, here we are." She inserted a large golden key into the door's oversized lock and turned it. There was a click. Katy then turned the key again, in the opposite direction. The whole apparatus clicked again, louder this time, then seemed to shudder inwardly. There were sounds of clockwork working inside it.

Slowly, the huge door opened inward with a hiss, and a puff of steam emerged from the hinges. They all held their breath. "Right," said Katy. "Come on in to…the vault!"

The small group tiptoed in, Katy setting about lighting a variety of small lanterns hanging from the walls. Slowly, the room started to light up and Alyssa beheld the repository of knowledge.

Her heart sank. The room was nowhere near as large or as extensively packed with books as she had expected. "This won't take long," she sighed.

"Give us a chance," said Katy. "There's a lot here."

They began to search.

ALYSSA

✝ ✝ ✝

Victoria chanced a peek through the open vault door and then ducked back.

Tracking the trio had taken a little doing; the library was vast. Fortunately, their hushed conversation carried unexpectedly well within the main library building, and the yell of "ouch" had aided her pursuit when they descended into the basement. The lantern light had helped as well, almost like a little guide light bobbing on an ocean.

She'd almost tripped over a discarded box of books, and nearly banged her head on a couple of wooden support pillars, but other than that nothing had hindered her in following them down here. All three of the youngsters were in the vault now, searching through the bookcases, apparently unaware of her presence.

She leaned against the wall down from the door and waited in the shadows, listening to the rustling of paper and the occasional muttering.

C H A P T E R   1 2

THE UNEXPECTED

With each discarded parchment, Alyssa's heart sank further. This was not what she had expected.

She had wanted to be searching a vast repository, one that would take hours, or even multiple visits, to go through; one that would maybe yield what she needed. Yield a cure, or a ritual or something.

Instead, she had a room no bigger than the ground floor of her home, with a few hundred books that they would search through in just a few hours, if that. It almost laughed in the face of the hope that Katy had ignited in her heart.

She dare not tell Katy her concerns. The girl thought she was helping.

She pulled out another book from the shelf she was reviewing. It had no title on the spine and its pages seemed fresher than many she had already checked through. She flicked through it but quickly found it was, in fact, an ancient ritual book from the Far East. For growing potatoes.

201

ALYSSA

Why is this even here?

She hung her head.

How many more disappointments will I endure tonight?

"Found something." James's voice came from behind a stack of books.

Alyssa glanced over. James was handling an aged book, a huge leather-bound one, dusty and practically ready to fall apart.

James had uttered the same words several times already.

"What is it?" she asked.

"A ritual," he said.

Another one. Wonder if this one will tell us how to make grass greener.

"Ritual to remove the vampire's blessing on the unworthy," he intoned, seeming to be reading from the book.

Alyssa frowned and wandered over. He held it out to let her read the page he was on. It was in a barely legible script, obviously an old book. Various symbols were dotted about the ageing page, but true enough, at the top were those very words.

"Should they that are given the blessing be found wanting," she read aloud with difficultly, the common tongue barely readable on the ancient pages, "and the punishment of True Death be found to be too harsh, the Master may taketh from them the blessing of our people."

Now I'm interested.

James let her take the book from him and she read with renewed vigour. Katy joined them.

"To do so, the Master must find for himself a virgin of either sex. By force or by trickery, they must make the accursed drink of the virgin's blood. Then, the accursed teeth must be shattered, broken apart into many pieces. In such a way, the blessing of the vampire is taken from the unholy and they shall revert to their mortal self."

Alyssa blinked. *It can't be that simple.*

She had been reading aloud the whole time; now she met the gazes of her two friends. James was the first to speak. "So, what it's saying is, drink the blood of a virgin, then shatter the teeth… and that's it?"

"According to this, yes." She looked over the verses again. "I don't know."

"What have you got to lose?" Katy asked.

"My teeth are what allow me to take blood, to sustain myself. Without them…" She shuddered.

Was this it? Was this the real thing? Was this the end?

She desperately wanted to believe it, desperately wanted to believe that this was the start of a new life. She read over the page again, then started to flick through the book. Quickly she realised this was something of a vampire "manual," one that seemed to have been copied from something much older; that explained the use of the common tongue.

She spotted instructions on how to feed, how to avoid sunlight, how to dream. For a moment she thought she had found how to turn someone into a vampire, but the pages had been torn out. *Maybe this is real.*

From her own experiences, the instructions in the book were all accurate. Some even had crude diagrams. Ancient vampire instructions. *Is it?* She looked at her friends.

Katy was the first to speak up. "What do you want to do, Alyssa?"

ALYSSA

Alyssa pursed her lips. Could she take the chance? Take the chance on this? Such a simple question, but now? Now when she had to make a choice?

A year and a half of waiting. Hoping. Living, after a fashion. Surviving. Enduring the Craving, the attentions of Vlad, the ever-present fear of going too far. Underestimating her strength. The fear of doing something that would really hurt someone.

Strange as it was, her memory reminded her of the mugger she had nearly killed; she hoped he was all right, despite his intentions. Was this at last a critical moment where she could change things? To change back? To become human again?

"All right," she said with an accompanying sigh of trepidation, catching herself off guard with how quickly she decided. "Let's try it."

"Yes, let's," came a voice.

The three of them spun round. James's lantern illuminated Victoria as she stood in the doorway of the room. She had a pistol drawn and aimed. "Hello again," Victoria greeted them without warmth.

"Ah, hey," replied Alyssa with an attendant nervous wave.

"Who might this be?" asked Victoria, stepping into the room but keeping her pistol primed and pointed at Alyssa. She directed her question at James. He didn't flinch. Alyssa was impressed.

"My name is James Fogan," he said, meeting Victoria's eyes. "I'm her boyfriend."

Alyssa did her best to hide her pride.

"Cute," remarked Victoria without emotion. "So," she said next, keeping a respectable distance from all three of them. "You've found a way to change her back?"

Alyssa and her friends exchanged glances. "Yes," Katy said.

"And you're going to do that right now?"

"Yes," James said.

"Right," said Victoria. "Won't be needing this then." She holstered her pistol. "So, how can I help?"

"You want to help us?" Alyssa asked.

"Don't look so surprised." Victoria took a more relaxed step toward the group. "You changing back into a human actually helps me."

"How?"

"You'll see. And don't get too happy," added Victoria, eyeing Alyssa. "I still owe you for blowing me into a snowdrift."

Alyssa gave Victoria an apologetic grin, but Victoria's expression remained neutral.

"Sorry about that," Alyssa said.

"Anyway, here's the deal, kids." Victoria outlined what was to happen. It generated a lot of surprised expressions, and a few raised eyebrows.

"That's your plan?" asked Katy, her eyes betraying uncertainty.

"Yes. Malak's not happy about it," she glanced at Alyssa, "but for you, it might offer your only way of living a normal life after this. That is, assuming you change back into a human. I caught what you were saying, but how's it going to work?"

Katy, with caution, passed the book to Victoria, and James kindly lifted the lantern so she could see properly. Victoria's eyes quickly scanned over the page. "Ouch," she concluded.

"Yes," agreed Alyssa. "I'm not looking forward to that. I'm not sure how we'll do it."

ALYSSA

Victoria drew her pistol again. "I'll do it." Alyssa gulped, and Victoria smiled confidently. "I'm an excellent shot. Next question, which virgin? 'Cause I'm not doing it."

Alyssa, Katy and James all managed to give Victoria the same look of surprise. Victoria glared back. "I was trying to be funny, okay?" she said. "Which virgin out of you two?"

She nodded to Katy and James. The two of them shuffled nervously. Alyssa didn't want to inflict it on either of them. That was, if they were both virgins.

"We can try eeny meany miny moe?" said Victoria with a smirk.

"Not helping," Alyssa said.

"Me." James stepped forward.

"And me." Katy did the same.

Alyssa caught Victoria rolling her eyes. "Youngsters, she needs just one of you."

Alyssa looked from one to the other before settling on Katy. "We'll need you to get us out of here if things don't go according to plan," she told her.

"Good luck," Victoria said, stepping back and giving Alyssa and James room.

The two of them stared at each other. "I love you," said Alyssa, "but please don't watch me when I do this. I..." She swallowed, her face down, not able to meet his gaze. "It's monstrous."

She felt a hand gently raise her chin and she stared into his eyes again. "If it gives you back your humanity," he said, "then I don't care. I'll do whatever it takes." He turned, exposing his neck and obediently closing his eyes.

† † †

Victoria watched as James closed his eyes.

The girl opened her mouth. Victoria watched as the fangs, the girl's terrible teeth, grew forth. She felt her finger tensing on her trigger and her pistol arm shuddered. She watched as the girl's face was twisted and warped by the growth of her canine teeth. With a suddenness that caught Victoria off guard, the girl pushed the fangs into her boyfriend's throat. Breathing through her nose, Alyssa drank her fill. The sound was not unlike someone downing a tankard, the girl gulping loudly and her throat swallowing down the life blood.

James, for his part, gasped, then seemed to just stand there taking it. Whether due to his bravery or what effect the fangs had on him wasn't obvious.

Alyssa pulled back as the deed was done.

Promptly, the lad fainted dead away.

"James!" Katy rushed to his side and Alyssa stepped back. Fear was in the girl's eyes, despite the fact that it was she who had done it. It hadn't taken that long.

Katy checked him, putting her ear to his chest. There was a tense moment when everyone held their breath. Victoria found her thumb hovering over her pistol's cocking hammer.

"He's okay," Katy said at last.

Victoria nodded, and Alyssa turned toward her. "Glim geady," she said with the oversized fangs still protruding. The girl opened her mouth wider, tilting back, the fangs glinting in the lantern light. Victoria moved to one side and brought her pistol round to aim at the side of the two extended canines.

ALYSSA

A single drop of blood dripped from the end of one of the teeth. Victoria took a deep breath. "Katy, stay down," she ordered.

Victoria and Alyssa stood still, and Katy ducked down by James who was still lying on the floor, out cold.

"Ready?" Victoria asked.

Alyssa nodded. Beads of sweat formed on the girl's forehead.

Victoria's hand gripped her pistol. For a brief moment, the lantern light caught the spiral of gold that coiled round the weapon's barrel. She pulled the cocking hammer back. The metallic click echoed around the room; Katy flinched at the sound and squeezed her eyes shut.

Victoria took a breath and steadied her aim. Alyssa's eyes closed. Victoria's eyes hardened to her task.

Her finger tightened on the trigger. Alyssa remained statue-still. Victoria breathed out, then in, holding her breath. She squeezed the trigger, and the pistol fired. The bang was deafening.

Her bullet hit Alyssa.

☦ ☦ ☦

For a split second Alyssa felt something against her teeth: a sudden hotness, boiling through them.

Then her world went black.

Alyssa's eyes opened again. She found herself on the floor of a dark room, its edges lost in shadow, its floor tiled white marble. Adjusting her glasses, she found a single light source above her, focused on her. She was not in her work clothes of the night but in her burgundy dress, one of her finer ones, clean and fresh.

This is odd.

Her hands leapt to her teeth and…

They were fine. She could feel her canines and there was nothing, nothing to indicate they had been shattered or otherwise broken. In fact, they felt normal, not quite as sharp and pointed. *Am I cured? Is it over?*

"No, my dear," said a deep rasping voice. "It is not over."

She stood up sharply, looking around for the source of the voice. "Who's there?" she called.

"Just an old friend," replied the voice mockingly.

The tone and accent did have a ring of familiarity about it, but Alyssa was finding it hard to place. "Do I know you?"

"Yes," it replied again, seeming to come from everywhere at once. "You refer to me as Vlad."

"Ah." Alyssa tried to find a cloud of annoying mouthy nothingness. "Where are you?"

Out of the darkness materialized not a cloud or a pair of red eyes, but instead, an armoured figure. A knight, of a sort. The metal armour he wore was ornately forged, a dull gold sheen glimmering where the light bounced off the sharp contours of its vambraces and pointed pauldrons. Worked into the metal were dozens of tiny pointed symbols, ragged and alien to her eyes; hung by the warrior's side was a thin sword sheath and dagger set cast in black leather. The armour was all-encompassing, the helm fashioned into what looked like the fanged maw of some carnivorous beast. A grill was set into the maw, covering the warrior's face. Only their eyes were visible through a thin slit just beneath the upper jaw. Two dark, authoritative eyes; dull red.

"I can see the cogs turning in your brain as you search your memories," the figure hissed. "Let me save you the bother. You referred to me as Vlad when you were unable to pronounce my true name," he explained. "That was intentional. After all, the vampiric tongue is ancient beyond most human years and takes decades to learn."

The figure reached up and undid his helmet clasp, lifting it off his head to cradle under one arm. The voice had sounded old, but the face from which it came was not. Young, but pale and refined. The age was behind the deep red eyes, not on the face.

More importantly, she recognised the face.

Alyssa felt her features pale. She knew him, ever since she had seen that same face disintegrate at the end of a bearkin long sword.

"Hello, my dear," said Igor Regorash with an accompanying smile. "It's so nice to see you again."

☩ ☩ ☩

"She's alive," Victoria confirmed. She had listened to Alyssa's chest and whilst the girl's heartbeat was weak, it was present. Even now, Victoria could see from the light of the lantern, some colour returning to the girl's features. The uncomfortable feeling Victoria experienced when around Alyssa had gone; there was no pressure or feeling of revulsion as she knelt by the girl. "Maybe this has worked," Victoria said to herself.

Alyssa's canine teeth, or at least what remained of them, were ruined and her face splattered with blood. Victoria's experience with her pistol had ensured that she fired just far enough away that the girl hadn't suffered any powder burns. The blood was from the teeth as they shattered.

James was looking on. His face was relieved but concerned.

He had awoken rapidly, and whilst weak, he now crouched nearby his unconscious beloved.

"She'll be okay, James, all right?" Victoria put her hand on the boy's shoulder. "We'll be able to get a healer to fix things."

He was still trembling, though whether by lack of blood or by shock Victoria couldn't tell. He nodded.

That's when Victoria heard them. The thunder of many feet.

"All right, you two," she said as she stood. "Keep behind me and shield Alyssa. Remember the plan. We need to delay them for as long as possible."

✝ ✝ ✝

"How?" Alyssa breathed.

Igor's smile remained.

"I knew my killers were on their way. Come to end my rightful reign, to ensure my destruction. I could not allow that, so I had my most trusted lieutenants perform a ritual. Something that, upon the destruction of my mortal body, would transfer my spirit to my most recent *convert*." He nodded toward her. "After which, I took on the persona of Vlad, so as to never raise your suspicions. If you had known it was me, I suspected you might not have been so accommodating. Sadly," he went on, his face turning irate, "you are a rather strong-willed soul, not accommodating at all! You were supposed to give in to me. Eventually, wearing your soul down, I would gain full unopposed control over your body and confine your soul to nothing but a weak memory. After that, another ritual would morph your body to my true form."

He motioned to his armoured self. "A God, reborn. Free

to bring this country to heel. But you were resistant, bluntly so, an unforeseen complication. But now," he waved to her with an armoured gauntlet, the fingers clicking as he opened his palm, "now you've given me an opportunity to correct that."

He let his helmet clatter to the floor, his face hardening as he reached to his sword belt. He slowly drew a long, thin blade with a resounding sound of steel on steel as the blade slipped easily past the sheath's ornate clasp.

Alyssa's eyes widened as she took a step back.

"By performing the ritual of *Unracos*, you've unwittingly given me *direct* access to your being. If I destroy your soul, I take possession of your body. And Igor Regorash will enter the world anew." He started to walk toward her, slowly, calmly and deliberately. "Now," he said, holding his blade at the ready, "hold still."

✝ ✝ ✝

There were a lot of them. Unfortunately, the room they were in was just about large enough for all of them. They'd swept in fast, taking positions along the length of the far wall. All facing toward her.

Victoria raised her hands, having holstered her pistol. Several crossbows were pointing at her. Horna Gladwell stared at her wearing a crooked grin, standing in the middle of the line of warriors. "I must congratulate you, Victoria," he said, peeking past her. "You've found our vampire." His expression darkened. "A pity you have been found in her company, if not her employ." He stepped forward to stand at the front of the line of Darnhun crossbows, regarding her.

"How'd you track us?" Victoria asked.

"It took us a little time," he said, clasping his hands behind his back and rocking from the heels to the balls of his feet. "But I am not without my own skills in investigation. I had already suspected something odd when you did not return from your pursuit." He started to pace in front of her. "Then, in a follow-up investigation, I discovered you had returned to the tavern. Apparently, you'd taken a chill during your hunt for the vampire. According to our contact, anyway."

He turned on his heel. "A young barmaid of the tavern in question. You had discovered the vampire but not captured it. An odd thing indeed. Considering you did not volunteer this information, naturally I assumed something else was going on and had one of the Darnhun follow you. They make effective scouts, by the way. They then summoned us here when you arrived and, here we are. At the end of the story."

"Which Darnhun?" Victoria hazarded.

Horna chuckled, nodding to one of the crossbow-wielding Darnhun. He gave a brief wave of acknowledgement before returning to his ready-to-fire stance.

"Yes. Hard to tell one from another, isn't it? Now," Horna went on, "I think we've wasted enough time. If you would kindly step out of the way." He removed a long, thin flintlock pistol from his cloak and aimed it at Victoria. "Right now."

Victoria, keeping her hands raised, moved to one side so that Horna could look at Alyssa's body. The girl lay cradled in Katy's arms, James holding one of her hands. They were both staring at Horna, eyes wide and faces pale.

Horna frowned. "And why is she in that state?" he asked.

213

"Seems these kids found something out about vampires," Victoria said.

Horna's frown did not lift. He kept his pistol aimed at Victoria. "Continue," he ordered.

"They discovered something from the books," she explained, nodding over at the stacks of bookcases. "Something that could change a vampire back to their human form."

"Continue," he said again, his eyes narrowing.

"It would be easier," she suggested tentatively, "if I could just show you. It's in one of the books. Over there. If you'll permit me?"

Horna smiled that crooked smile again. "Nice try, my dear." He used his other hand to signal to one of the Darnhun. Covered by his fellows, the soldier moved over to where Horna was, weapon up and aimed at the terrified youngsters at the centre of the room. "Which bookcase and which book? I will permit you to point without the need to shoot you. Yet," he added with relish.

Victoria pointed over to one of the bookcases. "Red book. Top left."

Horna looked over his shoulder and nodded. The soldier trotted over to the bookcase and started searching. Horna glanced over but kept his pistol trained on her. The Darnhun searched for a few seconds but presently turned around, shaking his head. Horna looked back at Victoria but she feigned ignorance.

He nodded to one of the other soldiers and indicated the same bookcase.

Two Darnhun now searched. Both Darnhun rapidly gave the same signal after a few moments. Horna stared back at Victoria again. He pulled the hammer back on his pistol with a loud click. "This is no time for games," Horna warned her.

✝ ✝ ✝

Alyssa backed away, keeping her distance as Regorash advanced. "I trusted you," she breathed, feeling her heart quicken. Quicken for the first time in a long time, but for all the wrong reasons.

"Yes, you did," he said. "That was a very stupid thing to do."

Suddenly, he lunged forward with his sword. An alarmingly sudden burst of speed. Alyssa, on instinct, stepped to one side. The blade just missed her by a hair's breadth.

"No less skilled. I can see you'll be an exercise at least."

She backed away again. Both of them were illuminated by the odd lights above them, the blackness they walked on seemingly infinite in all directions.

Where am I?

"We're in your head, you and I," Igor explained. "One soul against another. A thousand-year-old vampire, with decades of combat experience, and a legacy of strength and ability purified through generations of vampire ancestry." He nodded at her. "Against the teenage orphan girl. Unfair." He swung his sword in wide arcs, his grin turning cruel. "But that's life."

"How come I don't get a sword?" Alyssa said, playing for time as she narrowly managed to side-step another one of his thrusts.

"Have you ever used one?" he asked, ducking low and advancing on her, sword ready for another strike. "Have you thought about *having* a sword?"

"No."

Abruptly, a sword appeared in her hand. A fine legionnaire blade, a short sword. She'd seen it on the hips of militia watchmen.

ALYSSA
ALYSSA

She blinked in mute shock, but she recovered quickly, gripping the handle tightly and pointing the blade at him.

"Ah," he mused, smiling at her with a touch of praise. "I had forgotten that the so-called *dominant* soul has a certain amount of control over proceedings." He pointed his sword at her. "Use it," he goaded.

Alyssa looked from sword to Regorash and back again; she threw it at him.

Regorash rather easily ducked to one side and let the sword sail pass him to clatter into the darkness. He frowned as he glared back at her. "Generally, one uses a sword to parry and thrust, my dear. They make poor missiles." He straightened, as his eyes narrowed. "Time to die."

✝ ✝ ✝

"Fine. James, the book."

James flinched, glancing from Victoria to Horna. Horna kept his pistol on Victoria but nodded down at the boy.

"Just do it," said Victoria, her expression resigned.

James nodded, reaching behind him and bringing out the book. Horna smiled. "What a well-trained lad." He nodded to one of the Darnhun, who quickly moved over to snatch it off James. Horna holstered his pistol, and Victoria relaxed. "What page?" he asked as he was handed the book and began to flick through it.

"You really think I'll make it that easy for you?"

"After all that loyal service you have decided to turn on me?"

He continued leafing through the book, checking out each

216

page. Around him, the Darnhun kept watching. Victoria dared not move a muscle, and neither did Katy or James.

Or Alyssa.

✝ ✝ ✝

Alyssa backed away as Regorash took another swing. This time, he connected.

Mercifully for Alyssa, it only just broke the skin, a tear across her left arm, cutting through the sleeve of her tunic and drawing a sliver of blood. She winced, the feeling of pain a new experience.

He's playing with me.

"Yes, I am," agreed Regorash. "Technically, your arm should be hanging off. Give up, child. Even in your own mind, you have no hope."

"I do," she said, though without conviction.

How the hell am I going to beat this guy?

She thought of a sword and yet again, another appeared in her hand. Regorash, anticipating, swung his sword and Alyssa blocked clumsily. The momentum of the blow tore the sword from her hand, sending it clattering into the darkness.

"You can't fight me," he mocked.

Alyssa thought desperately. *How? How to beat him?* "All that time, you were lying to me?" she asked, trying to distract him.

"Yes," he replied without remorse.

"Even about the boxes?"

Regorash stopped, his face turning thoughtful. "An irritating distraction, I will admit."

Boxes.

217

In an eye-blink, a wooden box appeared between her and Regorash, complete with padlock. The exact one she had imagined countless times for containing Vlad. Igor grimaced.

"Just like that," he muttered with disgust, stepping around it.

Then another appeared, and another. Both identical, sitting in front of him, blocking his path.

"Novel, but merely a delaying tactic."

He used his free hand to swipe the nearest box out of his path, his immense strength sending it end over end into the shadows. He continued advancing on her. Another box appeared.

This time he kicked it, hard, smashing it asunder.

Two boxes, one above the other this time.

"What are you doing?" he demanded, knocking the boxes from his path. "You cannot win, you stupid girl!"

"No," she said.

Regorash blinked, momentarily stopping in his tracks.

Suddenly, Alyssa's stance became more confident. "You said this was *my* mind. That was your first mistake." She took a few steps toward him, and he frowned, flicking his blade out. "You said the boxes worked. That was your second mistake."

She stopped, just out of his weapon's reach. "And your third," she said, "was not backing off when I walked up to you."

Regorash lunged forward with blinding speed, his free hand closing around her neck and lifting her up. She gasped for breath, hands crawling at his gauntlet that now held her tightly, squeezing her throat.

"No, my dear," he sneered, holding Alyssa so far up that her feet dangled below her. "Walking up to me was *your* mistake."

He drew his sword back, angling it deliberately for a killing blow up into her heart. "This ends now."

A box slammed into him as if dropped from directly above him, bursting apart on impact in a shower of wood and shattered bricks. On a normal person, it would have crushed them flat. For Regorash, it was enough to distract him. He released Alyssa with a roar of anger and at the same time dropped his sword, staggering back. A hiss of anger issued from his lips.

Alyssa crumpled to the floor, gasping, as Regorash knelt to retrieve his sword.

"That was…"

Before he could recover his weapon, more heavy-laden wooden crates materialized from nowhere above and started to rain down on him. He tried to shield himself with his arms from the array of crates and containers. He hissed and snarled like a wild animal, momentarily ignoring Alyssa. He batted the boxes away or shattered them apart with his fists in a flurry of blows, but on and on the rain of material came, slamming into him with bone-crushing force, each bursting apart on impact and littering the area with debris.

Alyssa stood shaky, watching; she was angry. "You made me a monster," she spat. All her frustrations of the last eighteen months were boiling up, all her anger at being unable to lead a normal life.

Igor roared, rage now mixed with pain as Alyssa's hate was given physical form and hammered onto him. Each one of the boxes was weighted down, the shattered remains now lying about the weakening vampire lord in ever-increasing piles.

"You ruined my life. You took away the sunshine."

The deluge smashed into him now with even greater fury, as

if thrown instead of dropped. He growled through clenched teeth, having collapsed to the ground, his armour dented and pitted. The deep, dark magics of the armour, replicated in Alyssa's mind, were overwhelmed by the simple intensity of the bombardment.

"But I never followed your instructions."

She bent down and picked up his discarded sword as he rolled weakly on the floor nearby. The box bombardment ceased. It had done its work, he was beaten.

"I never killed anyone. Only took what blood I needed. Even helped those around me."

She advanced until she stood over him. He was battered and bruised, dazed and hardly moving now. His armour was buckled and broken in places, his chest plate caved in and covered in dust and wood chippings. His face was a mess, his forehead bloodied and his eyes bloodshot. It was no longer beautiful. Nearby, his discarded helmet still sat, the mouthpiece agape, as if in shock at the damage done to its wearer. She looked down on him, tears in her eyes.

"You ruined my life," she said again, "but I never stooped to your level. I never did anything evil."

He sneered at her though his battered features. "Nothing... evil," he mocked her, chuckling mirthlessly through his half-broken jaw, challenging her. "You can't...kill."

Her expression darkened. "With you, I'll make an exception."

His eyes widened. Alyssa breathed deeply, summoning all her strength, and then plunged the sword straight through his broken breast plate and into his heart. He had a moment to gasp, staring at the sword, his own sword, sticking out from his chest, its finely worked blade easily penetrating his damaged armour plate.

"Saw it in the book," she said, by way of explanation. "Just as good as a stake."

He made to reply but didn't get a chance as his body hissed and crackled around him. His body burned and popped as it turned to fire and ash. His flesh melted away, then his organs, before even his bones became as dust inside his armoured suit. The armour folded in on itself, the sword clattering to the floor as the metallic mass it had pierced evaporated to nothing. Then, even it crumbled to dust, the armour and sword rusting rapidly; not even the helm remained. Within seconds, all that was left was a pile of ashes amongst the debris of the boxes.

Alyssa watched it all. Tears in her eyes, heart aching and mind rebelling at the fact that however much he deserved it, she had just taken a life.

Exhaustion overcame her, and her world went black once more.

+ + +

Victoria heard movement behind her. Alyssa stirred, her eyes opening.

Horna tossed the book to one side and drew his pistol again. "You've been delaying me," he said bluntly through gritted teeth, his anger rising. He was now aiming his pistol toward Alyssa. Victoria, obediently, kept her arms up.

"Yes."

"The girl has changed back to a human," Horna stated.

"Yes." Victoria met his maddening gaze.

He was shaking now with rage. "You have ruined every-thing!" he bellowed.

Just at that moment, Victoria heard the sound of running feet. "Yeah," she said. "And guess what? I'm not finished."

"On the floor!" bellowed a strong northern Tornarian accent, as Malak and a group of Tornarian mercenaries and Larrick City militia men burst in from the corridor, weapons raised.

The mercenaries with Malak were dressed in a similar style to him, with utility leather battle plate and welding K-12 repeater crossbows. The militia men, in their blue and red tabards, each sin-gled out one of the Darnhun warriors, forcing them to the ground with aggressive words or batons. One by one, the Darnhun were knocked to the ground.

"Damn you!" Horna yelled, his pistol swinging round. He didn't know who to point at, his rage blinding him.

"Drop it now!" bellowed Malak, his K-12 and those of three of his brethren being quickly aimed in Horna's direction.

"Best do as he says, Horna," said a new voice, its volume thunderous and its tone commanding.

From behind the line of Tornarian mercenaries strode a tall, formidable figure clad in grey robes and red fur, his face covered by a thick ginger beard and his eyes a piercing blue. Kane Maldor, Master of the Internal Investigation Department.

Victoria could see fingers tensing on crossbow triggers.

Then Horna did something no-one expected. He aimed his pistol, but not at any of the mercenaries or even at Victoria; he aimed for Alyssa. He pulled the hammer back, his eyes wide with rage.

Victoria dived for the pistol.

Horna's weapon fired.

CHAPTER 13

THE RIGHT
KIND OF ENDING

Victoria's eyes flickered open. Immediately, she shut them again. "Gods," she groaned. "Turn off the light!"

"Victoria!" It was Malak's voice.

"Malak," she said weakly. "What the…?"

"You," he was saying, though she couldn't see him, "are one bloody lucky woman. Proper stupid one as well."

"I aim to please," she admitted, her head groggy; she rubbed her eyes with her right arm. "What happened?"

"You took a bullet that was going for the girl. Went straight through your arm. You've been out most of the day."

"Yay for me," she replied without enthusiasm, now registering a dull pain in her left arm. "Ouch, that hurts."

As her eyes started to focus, she found she was in a long room with beds arrayed on either side. Malak sat beside her, several mead mugs beside him on a small table and a pillowcase propped by the bed. As she became used to the light of the window in front of her, Victoria found her arm was in a sling and she was dressed in bedclothes.

ALYSSA

"Horna?"

Victoria's eyes had focused enough to see Malak grinning.

"Oh yeah, took the bastard myself. He survived, but it won't be a good life. Which was an accident, you understand," he added quickly, his expression mock serious. "I just happened to shoot him right in the base of his spine."

"Accidents do happen," she agreed. She grimaced slightly, feeling her injured arm. "I take it the Internal Investigation Department will…"

"Press charges, oh yes. He'll hang regardless. Or worse."

"Glynis?" Victoria asked.

"Kane gave her immunity, I think, same for you. It sounds like it's going to be a big case."

"What about the girl?" Victoria asked.

Malak nodded across to the other side of Victoria's bed. "See for yourself."

There across from her was Alyssa, looking back at her. She wasn't in a position to talk, though, as her mouth was covered by a thick bandage. She could already tell the girl had changed. Her cheeks were reddened instead of pale, and she had seemingly chosen the most well-lit area of the dormitory. Alyssa nodded over at the window from which bright sunshine came straight down on top of her and looked back at Victoria.

Victoria nodded.

"We did good, I think," Malak said, smiling over first at Alyssa, then toward Victoria as she turned back to him. "We did real good."

☩ ☩ ☩

Around her, everyone and anyone was talking, dancing and drinking across the length and breadth of the tavern. The music was loud from a group of bards in the corner, the ambience cheery and the company plentiful. Malak was over to one side, regaling some of the attractive young barmaids on his momentous adventures.

Gretna, unable to stop working, had at least a mug of mead in one hand as she cleaned tables and barked orders on the other side of the busy tavern.

Katy was being courted by a young militia man, grinning from ear to ear and letting her pigtails bob from side to side.

James was in his element, surrounded by a cohort of militia men and engineers. He looked no longer as shy as Victoria had seen him.

She and Alyssa had gotten out of the healing wards at the same time. James had arrived to escort Alyssa into the light of the day. The bandages had hidden the girl's smile but Victoria had known it was there; the way the girl craned up, not even bothering to shield her eyes as she beheld the bright winter sunlight. Malak and Victoria had looked on.

"Now that," Malak had pointed to the young couple as they had walked off, hand in hand, "that's what we're working for, isn't it? That's 'the peace.' Freedom to enjoy life."

"You sentimental sod," Victoria had said with admiration in her voice. "You are exactly right."

Victoria now sighed and sipped her wine.

"Hey." Alyssa stood beside her. The girl no longer had a deathly pale face. The bandage had been removed, allowing a beautiful smile to shine.

Victoria nodded. "Hey," she said and, after checking that

those nearby were not looking her way, returned the smile fleetingly. "I see the healers did a fine job on your teeth."

Alyssa nodded, her hand moving to her mouth. "It feels… normal. What about your arm?"

Victoria sighed. "I'm allergic to healing potions, so it'll just have to heal the old-fashioned way."

Alyssa nodded. "I never properly thanked you," she said, with a twinge of nervousness in her voice.

"It's my job." Victoria shrugged. "Keeper of the peace and all that."

"Yeah, but still…" Alyssa paused, as if searching for her next words. Quite unexpectedly, she practically leapt on top of Victoria to hug her tightly.

Victoria flinched, then returned the embrace. "It's okay," she said, "it's over now."

Alyssa cried into Victoria's good shoulder, the occasional "thank you" muffled between sobs.

Victoria patted the girl's back with difficulty, having to use her wounded arm. "Yeah, I know. Let it out."

Alyssa did just that as Victoria's hand moved up and down the girl's back. She was shuddering as her body released the tension.

"It's been a long time for you, I know," Victoria said. "A long time for such a curse."

Eventually, the girl broke off, sniffing and wiping her eyes. "Sorry about that. You were right, that…that was a long time coming."

Victoria nodded.

It was only then that they both became aware that the noise in the tavern had suddenly dropped.

Slowly, Victoria looked around. Her eyes widened as she noticed every single pair of eyes now on her and Alyssa. Malak was smirking at the far end of the room.

"Three cheers for the hero!" bellowed Gretna across the bar.

Across the tavern, mugs were raised and voices cheered.

Victoria waved, half-heartedly, with her good arm. Alyssa looked around with wide eyes. "Ah," she began, leaning in to whisper in Victoria's ear. "They're cheering us, aren't they?"

"Yes. Yes, they are."

Gretna strode over as the cheers continued. "Get up, the both of you!" she ordered. "Take a bow for Grogra's sake!"

Alyssa resumed standing awkwardly and Victoria wasn't given much of a choice as Gretna rather cruelly used the injured arm to help her out of her seat. "Ouch! This is your fault," hissed Victoria though a forced smile and a red face, though without menace.

"Sorry!" whispered Alyssa, her cheeks burning. "How long do you think they'll make us stand?"

"Till they get bored," replied Victoria.

It took two agonisingly long minutes for the final clapping and cheering to end, the continuation prompted mostly by Malak. He approached Victoria as the clapping abated. "I will never let you live this down," he warned with a superior smirk.

"Really?" She took her goblet and downed the remains of her drink in a single long gulp. "Wrong answer." With a speed that took the entire room off guard, she took his face in hand and brought him in for a long, passionate, and forceful kiss. One that left his eyes bulging and his mouth agape.

"Now we're even," she said with smug satisfaction. "Proper even."

ALYSSA

The whole room whooped in excitement, except of course the barmaids Malak had left behind at the other end of the bar.

"He said he was single!" one of them piped up as Victoria swooped past them to the bar.

Gretna nodded as she passed. They both exchanged grins.

"Nicely done." Gretna nodded her approval again. "Very nicely done."

✝ ✝ ✝

Alyssa slipped away, back into the corner of the tavern, straight into James's arms. The kiss they shared was just as passionate, if not more so than the one Victoria and Malak had shared. She took James's face in her hands, looking intently into his eyes. "I am truly, truly happy," she said. "Now," she said after a few more glorious moments of kissing her beloved. "I'm hungry."

WATCHER IN THE NIGHT

The two figures watched from across the street.

Both clad all in black, one in a golden mask beneath his hood, the other's features lost in shadow. No one noticed them as patrons entered and exited the tavern. The light of the tavern candles did not seem to touch them.

"The test has been completed," intoned the faceless one, disappointment evident in his gruff tone. "The rival eliminated. The mark found to be wanting." He chuckled without humour. "A pity; another ally would have been most useful. Still, killing the drunk has yielded a great deal of unexpected information."

"Yes, Leader," agreed the golden-masked man.

"Horna Gladwell's alliance with the Darnhun, for example, is closer than expected." The faceless one's voice darkened. "I trust you did not withhold *that* information from me?"

"No, no, I swear!" The masked man looked to the other, flinching back. The other figure's form seemed to rise up. As if beneath his cloak, he grew larger. Tendrils of blackness rippled from under the cloak, shooting outwards to coil around the other man's all-too-human feet.

"Swear it," his master demanded in a low growl, his voice carrying a deep edge of malice; around him, the shadows darkened, boiling and shifting.

"I swear it!" gasped the other, rooted to the spot. "I did not know my brother was so well-connected!"

For tense seconds the faceless individual continued to swell, moving close to his companion. Then, suddenly, the form receded again. The blackness around him evaporated; the tendrils retracted. He became once again just a man in a cloak. "Very well," he said simply, his voice returning to normal.

He glanced back toward the tavern. "The Council of Peace Investigators were diligent indeed," the Leader continued. "Even when we had arranged for the railings to be removed so swiftly, they rose to that challenge." He nodded at his own conclusions. "Admirable and interesting to see not one, but two individuals immune to the aura." He inclined his head, nodding to the other man who was now suitably cowed. "That was not just a coincidence. Perhaps such humans are more widespread than at first believed. If we could locate more, they would prove useful in the future."

The faceless figure promptly turned and started to float back down the alleyway. The masked man moved to follow on unsteady legs.

"Come," the Leader commanded. "We have work to do."

HALDRED CHRONICLES
BOOK 2: KALLA

"You will find peace a hard thing to keep"
Kalla is a ghost, and until recently she was quite happy in that vocation. Then the place she was haunting exploded. She suddenly finds herself a prime witness to the incident and is left wondering what to do. Dare she interact with the mortal realm to help out the living?

Victoria Haldred has recovered from her wounds and is keen to get back to work. Assigned to investigate the collapse of an important bank, she soon discovers it's not just a case of shoddy construction work.

Kalla and Victoria each posses half the truth. Will they cooperate to bring things to a head, before the collapse of a bank becomes the least of their worries?

Time is against them, and evil forces bent on bringing the world back to a state of total war are moving, and moving fast.

ACKNOWLEDGMENTS

This is my first novel, and hopefully depending on how it is received, not my only one.

There are a lot of people who have contributed time and effort to helping me produce this. Not least of which are my elite cadre of very patient proofreaders and beta readers who even as they are finishing reading this acknowledgement will be having painful flashbacks to some truly awful grammar and spelling mistakes from previous drafts.

All being well, these have now been eliminated in this final product. Barrie, Mat, Carson, David, Cynthia, Cara, Lesley-Anne, Gail, Esther, Andrew, Robert, Michael, Christopher, Deborah, Katrina, and Lucy. To you all I say, thank you so very much for all your time and effort. For the immense amount of work they put into helping me with this novel, everything from scene suggestions to correcting spelling mistakes to full-blown reviews.

Most recently, I must acknowledge the exceptionally talented work of Brad Pauquette and the editors of Boyle and

ALYSSA

Dalton. Brad's detailed, professional editing of this book has been of immense help not only with the story itself but in shaping the series from this moment onwards. The additional work by Boyle and Dalton themselves has finalised this story.

Finally, many, many other friends, work colleagues, and family members have offered advice and encouragement in the completion of this book. Whether it was a scene suggestion, a character sketch or just a "keep it up JG," to you all, thank you for helping me to at last, finish this novel.

I hope you, the reader, whoever you are, will have enjoyed this little attempt at urban fantasy.

ABOUT THE AUTHOR

JG Cully lives and works in Northern Ireland. His healthy obsession with wargaming and tabletop role-play games eventually led him to write his own stories. He has been writing fantasy books since 2012, and he completed his first full novel as part of the November writing challenge "Nanowrimo." He is husband to a supportive wife and father to an energetic five-year-old and one-year-old.

His urban fantasy series *Haldred Chronicles* is set in a post-war world and follows the investigations of Victoria Haldred, a Council of Peace investigator, as she battles to maintain a fragile peace.

ALYSSA

BLOG PAGE
jgswritinganovel.blogspot.co.uk

GOODREADS PAGE
goodreads.com/jgcully

JG'S AUTHOR PAGE (US)
amazon.com/author/jgcully

HALDRED CHRONICLES FACEBOOK PAGE
facebook.com/haldredchronicles

TWITTER
twitter.com/jgwritesnovels

LINKEDIN
uk.linkedin.com/jgcully

PINTEREST
pinterest.com/jgcully

TUMBLR
tumblr.com/blog/jgcully

INSTAGRAM
instagram.com/jg_cully